The Short Stories of William Pett Ridge

William Pett Ridge was born at Chartham, near Canterbury, Kent, on 22nd April 1859.

His family's resources were certainly limited. His father was a railway porter, and the young Pett Ridge, after schooling in Marden, Kent became a clerk in a railway clearing-house. The hours were long and arduous, but self-improvement was Pett Ridge's goal. After working from nine until seven o'clock he would attend evening classes at Birkbeck Literary and Scientific Institute and then to follow his passion; the ambition to write. He was heavily influenced by Dickens and several critics thought he had the capability to be his successor.

From 1891 many of his humourous sketches were published in the St James's Gazette, the Idler, Windsor Magazine and other literary periodicals of the day.

Pett Ridge published his first novel in 1895, A Clever Wife. By the advent of his fifth novel, Mord Em'ly, a mere three years later in 1898, his success was obvious. His writing was written from the perspective of those born with no privilege and relied on his great talent to find humour and sympathy in his portrayal of working class life.

Today Pett Ridge and other East End novelists including Arthur Nevinson, Arthur Morrison and Edwin Pugh are being grouped together as the Cockney Novelists.

In 1924, Pugh set out his recollections of Pett Ridge from the 1890s: "I see him most clearly, as he was in those days, through a blue haze of tobacco smoke. We used sometimes to travel together from Waterloo to Worcester Park on our way to spend a Saturday afternoon and evening with H. G. Wells. Pett Ridge does not know it, but it was through watching him fill his pipe, as he sat opposite me in a stuffy little railway compartment, that I completed my own education as a smoker... Pett Ridge had a small, dark, rather spiky moustache in those days, and thick, dark, sleek hair which is perhaps not quite so thick or dark, though hardly less sleek nowadays than it was then".

With his success, on the back of his prolific output and commercial success, Pett Ridge gave generously of both time and money to charity. In 1907 he founded the Babies Home at Hoxton. This was one of several organisations that he supported that had the welfare of children as their mission.

His circle considered Pett Ridge to be one of life's natural bachelors. In 1909 they were rather surprised therefore when he married Olga Hentschel.

As the 1920's arrived Pett Ridge added to his popularity with the movies. Four of his books were adapted into films.

Pett Ridge now found the peak of his fame had passed. Although he still managed to produce a book a year he was falling out of fashion and favour with the reading public and his popularity declined rapidly. His canon runs to over sixty novels and short-story collections as well as many pieces for magazines and periodicals.

William Pett Ridge died, on 29th September 1930, at his home, Ampthill, Willow Grove, Chislehurst, at the age of 71.

He was cremated at West Norwood on 2nd October 1930.

Index of Contents

THE ALTERATION IN MR. KERSHAW

"I've knocked about a pretty tidy bit in my time—I'm as much as fifteen next birthday—and I don't write this story from the standpoint of a man who is ignorant of the world. I'm wonderfully observant, and I take notice of little incidents sometimes in a way that surprises even myself. Incidents, I mean, that other people overlook. The junior partner called me the other evening a sharp lad, and 'pon my word he wasn't far wrong. I don't wish to brag about it; I only wish to hint that what I don't notice isn't worth noticing. I've picked out a horse sometimes, and I've—But I want to tell you about Mr. Kershaw.

Mr. Kershaw is one of the senior clerks in our office; he's the one with rather rough hair, and a collar turned down low all the way round. Most of the clerks are smart and wear high collars, and they wear neckties too that make me gasp. All nice gentlemanly fellows they were when I first came here, bar Mr. Kershaw. Mr. Kershaw was what I call a terror.

"Billing, why aren't these inkstands seen to?"

"Beg pardon, sir, but—"

"I've had to speak to you before about this, Billing."

"I can't do forty thousand things a minute, sir."

"Another word of your confounded insolence, and I shall ask the firm to dispense with your services."

"That ain't insolence, sir, it's simply a fact. If I want to be insolent I know a lot of words—"

"Go away, Billing! You're a perfect nuisance in the place. I shall take an early opportunity of asking the firm to look out for a decent lad."

That's the sort of thing that went on day after day, me and Mr. Kershaw going at it hammer and tongs. I should have got really cross about it only that Mr. Kershaw was just the same with all the others, especially with the juniors. The grumpiest man, I venture to say, that ever came up to the City from Dulwich on a morning since the line's been opened.

One July Mr, Kershaw went away for his three weeks' holiday, and when he came back, the first news was that he was married.

"Now," I said to Linkson, who copies the letters, "now you mark my words. Old K. 'll change his manner."

"For better or for worse?" asked Linkson. "There's something wrong with our copying-ink. This letter hasn't come out a bit clear."

"Whether for better or worse," I answered, "I can't tell you. Sometimes getting spliced has one effect; sometimes the other. But I'll bet you as much as three'apence that we shall notice an alteration."

"I've half a mind to take you," said young Linkson, doubtfully, "only I've got a good deal of money out just now. I've backed Swiftsure for twopence, one, two, three."

"Take it or leave it," I said. "It's an offer, and if you're not sportsman enough to have a bet on, don't."

"She's pretty, they say," remarked Linkson. He gave a twist to the copying press and looked narrowly at Mr. Kershaw hanging up his hat and smoothing his rough hair. "One of the young partners said she was as neat a little figure as ever—"

"Billing," shouted Mr. Kershaw furiously from his office, "come here at once."

To save argument, I went.

"Will you be good enough to explain," demanded Mr. Kershaw, hotly, "to explain, Billing, the condition of this table? Look here! I can write my name on it."

"So could I, sir," I said. "There's nothing clever in that."

"Why on earth isn't the place dusted properly," he shouted. "Why do I come back here—"

"'Eaven knows!" muttered.

"And find the place neglected in this manner? Get a duster at once."

"Right, sir."

"But it is not right, Billing," he declared.

"Very good, sir," I said, "it's wrong. I'll fetch the duster in 'alf a tick. But first of all I 'ope it won't seem out of place if I congratulate you, sir, on what I may term a recent matrimonial event."

"Get a duster at once. Billing," he said, sharply, "and don't let us have quite so much talk. It's not business."

I felt very glad that Linkson hadn't booked that bet of threehalfpence, because I most certainly should have lost. So far from Mr. Kershaw's marriage improving his temper, I'm not at all sure that it wasn't worse. I used to say to Linkson I hoped he didn't carry on like that at home, and Linkson—he knows a lot, Linkson, although he's only a little bit of a chap—Linkson used to answer that men who had their tantrums in the City, were generally men who were not allowed to show them in their own homes. But, somehow, I'd an idea that this was not the case with Mr, Kershaw.

About twelve months after his marriage the alteration that I want to tell you about came. I was the first to notice it, and I passed the news round the office. There happened to be a new baby at my place, and I wanted the afternoon off to see some people my mother washes for. What does Mr. Kershaw do but look up from his table quite cheerfully and say,

"By all means. Billing."

"Much obliged to you, sir,

"Going to take your young lady out for the day, Billing?"

I never saw Mr. Kershaw smile before, and upon my word it took my breath away for a moment.

"No, sir," I said, "I've broke it all off with her."

"Sorry to hear that."

"Fact of the matter is, sir, she was a bit too fond of fourpenny ices. Turned up her nose, bless you, at two penny ones. Would have four pennies. And when you begin to shell out fourpence after fourpence, and see her getting less imbibe at each ice, why—"

"It is not with her, then, that you wish to spend the afternoon?"

I explained, and Mr. Kershaw rose from his chair and sat on the corner of the table, just as though he was the most cheerful gentleman in the City.

"Why, that's singular!" he said, good-temperedly.

"I don't know about that, sir," I answered. "There's nine of us already."

"But what I mean to say, it's odd. Because, do you know. Billing, I have a little arrival at home. And that's a boy, too."

"Fine boy, sir, may I ask?"

"As fine a little man," said Mr. Kershaw, enthusiastically, "as ever came into this world. Bright-eyed, healthy, chubby—perfect picture of a boy. I don't suppose, as a matter of fact, that such a perfect youngster is often seen. He's got a way of staring fixedly at one—"

Mr. Kershaw this time absolutely laughed. I went to the door.

"I say, Billing. I should like to give your new brother something. Has he got a mug?"

"He's got a rare funny little mug, sir," I answered. "We all pinch his little nose for him, but unless he alters he won't be what I call dazzlin' 'andsome."

"I mean a silver christening mug," explained Mr. Kershaw. "If not, you must let me present him with one. Good morning, Billing."

It wasn't believed in the office at first, but the clerks soon saw that the change was real. Linkson declared that he overheard Mr. Kershaw one evening, just before he left the office, humming a comic song; Linkson admitted that Mr. Kershaw hummed it all wrong, but still he hummed it. One of our clerks lived at Slough, and Mr. Kershaw called him in one day to ascertain his opinion of Eton as a school for a growing youth. The Slough clerk said that he had heard that Eton wasn't half a bad place, and Mr. Kershaw thanked him, and made a note of it in his diary. On another occasion, when the managing clerk to a solicitor's in Ely Place called at the office, Mr. Kershaw had a long conversation with him on the Bar as a profession for young men, and the chances it offered of advancement. I think that upon this point Mr. Kershaw was not quite decided, because I noticed on his blotting-pad a scribbled line.

"Bar. Query? Enquire re Church. See Canon Weste."

And underneath.

"Is Sandhurst expensive? Query? Tenth Hussars."

One day I posted a letter for him to a Sunday paper, and I got Linkson to persuade his father to buy a copy. In the "Answers to Correspondents" we found:

"Wahsrek.—In answer to your enquiry, I do not recommend a political career for your son, unless he shows a special ability for speaking and a thorough grasp of the great questions of the day. But if he decides to enter St. Stephen's, let him first read all John Stuart Mills's works and my own book called Customs and Habits of the Laplanders."

Somehow the whole office seem to be infected by the alteration in Mr. Kershaw. Everybody became a little more friendly with everybody, and when Master Kershaw was six months old and a proposal was made to send a birthday present to the little baby, the suggestion was taken up like one o'clock. Mr. Pascoe took the big basket of hot-house flowers into Mr. Kershaw's room, and presented it to Mr. Kershaw, and Mr. Kershaw came out into the office and shook hands with all of us, right down to me.

"Gentlemen," said he, as he stood at the door of his office, "I wish I could tell you how deeply I am touched by your kind thought of my—of my son. I shall take this delightful basket of flowers home with me this evening, and I shall tell my boy that although he is only six months old to-day, yet he has—he has friends who wish him well, and look forward with interest, and I hope I may say with affection, to the—to the time when—"

And here Mr. Kershaw suddenly broke down, went hurriedly into his office, and closed the door. Later he went off radiant, with the basket of expensive flowers, carried with great care.

The next morning Mr. Kershaw was an hour late coming to the office. This had never happened before within my knowledge, and there were a good many jokes going round the office about it. I remember that I made one or two of the best of them. When he did arrive he walked straight to his office and turned the key.

"Headache after the jollification last night," said the office.

My mother called round that morning with the baby. I don't believe in women-folk coming into the City at all, but mother was so excited about father having got a good berth that she said (you know what women are) that she felt as though she must come straight down and tell me the news. I knocked at the door of Mr. Kershaw's office, and he unlocked it.

"Beg pardon, sir, for troubling you, but my mother and the baby—anything the matter, sir?"

"Go on, Billing," he said, and turned his head away.

"They've just called, and I thought perhaps you wouldn't mind if I slipped out for a few minutes to show mother and baby the Tower Bridge."

"Billing!"

"Sir?"

"Do you mind—do you mind bringing your baby in here for a moment?" He coughed as though there was something in his throat, "I should rather like to see him."

"Only too proud, sir."

I brought the baby in myself, because I was afraid mother would drop her aitches or make me look silly in some way. I sat the little beggar on the table, and I'm blest if he didn't put out both his chubby arms to Mr. Kershaw. Fact!

"I expect he ain't the baby yours is, sir," I remarked respectfully. Mr. Kershaw was patting the tiny chin and whispering baby-talk to the little kid.

"No, Billing," he said. "No." He turned away again so that I couldn't see his face, and kissed our baby. "My boy—er—died last night."

What I want to add is, that Mr. Kersaw has never been the one he was in the old days. He's as kind mannered a senior clerk as you'll find between Temple Bar and Aldgate. And I've noticed that in the street sometimes, when a baby goes by and he catches sight of it, Mr. Kershaw will stop—it don't matter who he's with—and he will watch it until it goes right out of sight.

A CAUTIOUS YOUTH

Mr. George Wraight had, after great consideration, asked Miss Betterton to come up the river on the Cardinal Wolsey, and little Miss Betterton, after some coy hesitancy, and some debate with Miss Oliffe who shared her room over Oliffe & Oliffe's, had decided to accept it. Miss Oliffe had strongly urged that the invitation should be declined, and this had settled the matter.

"You shouldn't ask my advice, dear," said Miss Oliffe, tartly, "if you didn't mean to take it. Mr. Wraight's a very nice gentleman, and he parts his hair in the middle, and always lifts his hat in a well-bred manner, but I don't think it's the correct thing to go out with any gentleman unless—"

"That's just why I'm doing it, dear."

"You'll find out your mistake someday," said Miss Oliffe, punching her pillow with some annoyance. "Mark my words."

"It isn't as though I was like some girls," urged little Miss Betterton. "I'm not silly."

"So you say, dear."

"Are you fond of Mr. Wraight, Oliffe?"

"I wouldn't accept him," said Miss Oliffe, vehemently, "not if he went down on his bended knees. Have you said your prayers?"

There was equal tumult in the mind of Mr. Wraight in regard to the river trip. The idea had come suddenly to Mr. Wraight that being quite twenty-two the time was approaching when it would be wise to settle down and compose himself for married life. This was partly suggested by the fact that an uncle had generously offered to set him up in business in Hackney.

"She's the only girl I ever had the least 'ankering after," said Mr. Wraight to his looking-glass, "and I suppose I can't do better than offer her my 'and and my 'eart. But I shall be as cautious as I can, and the leastest thing will put me off."

It really seemed that everything promised well. At the Old Swan Pier was Miss Flora Betterton, looking much prettier in the eyes of Mr. Wraight than any young person had ever been permitted in this world hitherto to look, and a hat that was perfectly bewildering, Mr. Wraight's hand shook as he purchased tickets at the wooden office; when, down on the pier, Miss Betterton began in her bright decided way to talk, he was forced to hold tightly, with his brown gloved hand, the iron chain, to prevent himself from falling, in consequence of dizziness, into the water.

"The oddest thing!" exclaimed Miss Betterton. "Just along in Lower Thames Street—do you mind doing up this last button of my glove, Mr. Wraight? It is so difficult, you can't think—along in Lower Thames Street, who should I come across but Mr. Mervale."

"Ho!" said Mr. Wraight. "This button won't fasten. Your arm's too plump."

"My arm's all right," said Miss Betterton, "it's the glove that's wrong. What was I talking about?"

"You were saying—"

"Oh, I remember! About Mr. Mervale. Well, he's just over from South Africa on a holiday, you know."

"I didn't know," said George, rather gruffly. "Don't know the man from Adam."

"I'll introduce you presently," said Miss Betterton. "I expect he's gone down to the other end of the boat. You'll like him awfully; he's grown so good-looking."

"Good looks ain't everything," remarked George.

"We used to be in an elocution class together," went on Miss Bettorton, beamingly. "You don't go in for reciting do you, Mr. Wraight?"

"Singin's my line," said George.

"I suppose there'll be something of the kind going on as we come back. If I'm asked— Oh, the boat's moving!"

"I've got something I want to ask you presently," said George.

"I'm the worst one you ever met for riddles," she said. "I only know that one about 'When is a jar not a—'"

"It isn't exactly a riddle," explained George, awkwardly. "It's more important than any riddles; perhaps, if it's quite agreeable, I'll mention it on the return journey."

"Just as you like," said Miss Betterton agreeably. "We've got all the afternoon before us. I'm glad there's an orchestra on board, aren't you? I wouldn't give a penny for the river if it wasn't for the music on board."

"Music 'ath charms," quoted George with an effort, "to soothe the savage breast."

"Indeed," said Miss Betterton, coldly, a little hurt at the remark.

"Don't misunderstand me," said George, anxiously. "I wasn't arguing for a single moment that you—"

"Here's Mr. Mervale. Let me introduce you."

Mervale, a tall, clipped-bearded man with a Kentish accent and a quiet manner, said he was pleased to meet George, and George said (but his looks did not corroborate the statement) that he was proud to make the acquaintance of Mervale.

Mervale offered George his cigar-case, and George selected two, placing one in his waistcoat pocket to smoke, as he said, some other time. It was impossible to deny that Mervale was, if a silent, yet and attentive man. Just as George was thinking over the matter of refreshments, Mervale went below and returned with lemonade and claret for Miss Betterton; when the idea of going to the side of the vessel the better to see the Houses of Parliament struck him, he found that Mervale was already conducting the lady thither.

"Seems to me," said George, sitting back on his seat, "that I'm getting left. I shall have to set about this matter seriously."

A sheet of letter paper lay at George's foot. He picked it up absently, and closing his eyes thought out the form of declaration. By the time Miss Betterton had returned to her seat, George had made up his mind.

"Miss Betterton," he said, twisting the slip of paper nervously, "that little matter that I mentioned just now. Have you ever thought about getting married?"

Miss Betterton turned her pretty head away modestly.

"I don't know that I've ever paid much attention to the subject," she said.

"Well," urged George, "it's just as well to look these unpleasant facts—what I mean to say, it's no use putting everything off till the last moment."

"There's certainly something in that," agreed Miss Betterton. She arranged the lace edging of her scarlet parasol with exceeding care, "My mother always used to warn us girls against procrastination."

"Against who?" enquired George, sharply. Miss Betterton explained. "Oh, I see what you mean. But what I was speaking of, and what I wanted—what I wanted to ask you was—"

George assures me on his honor as a draper and a man, that a glass of water—nay, a mere sip of water at that moment would have saved him. His mouth seemed parched, his tongue unwilling. Nervously he unrolled the twisted sheet of note-paper and glanced at it. The writing was that of the decorous young lady beside him, and the first lines read thus:

"'Alfonso, dearest, why do you remain away from everyone that holds you dear? I, who desire your presence near to me, would fain lay down my life to see thine eyes. Come—' "

George read no more. He crumpled the paper hastily, and the young lady turned to him.

"What you wanted to ask me was what?" enquired Miss Betterton.

"'Pon me word, I forget," declared George, lamely, "My memory's going like anything. I shall forget me own name presently."

"But can't you try to remember?"

George rubbed the top of his straw hat as one endeavouring to stimulate thought, and frowned at Blackfriars Bridge.

"It's gone," he said, despairingly.

"Perhaps you'll think of it again presently," suggested Miss Betterton, with some coyness.

"Perhaps," answered George. He folded the sheet of note-paper. "I fancy," he said, meaningly, "that this belongs to you."

Miss Betterton flushed with great confusion, and, taking the sheet hastily, placed it in her pocket at the back of her white skirt.

"How careless of me," she said, with much annoyance. "I am stupid. Have I just dropped it? I wouldn't have you look at that for worlds."

George went to the stern of the steamboat to smoke a cigar with the satisfied air of a man who has stopped himself on the very brink of a precipice, and Mervale from South Africa took his place.

"Pulled meself up," said George to himself, "just in time. Another moment and I should have been let in for it."

It was an awkward day for George, but it might have been much worse. To have ascertained the perfidy of Miss Betterton, and to have been forced to wear during the whole of the day a domino of geniality would have been intolerable. The fortunate presence on the voyage of Mervale—who really seemed a very decent, quiet, generous sort of fellow—enabled George, when he could no longer keep up the pretence of good temper, to leave Miss Betterton in the care of the man from South Africa, returning when his equanimity was temporarily restored. Such was George's thankfulness to Mervale, that he determined to disclose to him the information concerning Miss Betterton's foreign friend in order to place him upon his guard.

"You are dull all at once, Mr. Wraight," complained Miss Betterton. "When we started you were quite bright. Does the river journey upset you?"

"No," said George, curtly, "it don't."

"That's Richmond Park over there, isn't it? Be nice to go there some day, wouldn't it? A fine afternoon it would be rather pleasant."

"All right for them that like it."

"I believe you're almost a bit of a cynic, Mr. Wraight," said Miss Betterton, with an attractive air of reproof.

"It's enough to make anybody," said George, gloomily.

"I wish you'd tell me what it is that's gone wrong, I'm sure there's something."

"I tell you there isn't," said George, doggedly.

"You're not cross—you're not put at all because I'm speaking to Mr. Mervale? You see he's such an old friend."

"I don't mind you talking to him," declared George, honestly. "Seems a straightforward sort of chap enough."

"Well, then," persisted Miss Betterton, "it must be something else. Is it anything I've said?"

"Look 'ere," said George, goaded to desperation, "you let things be as they are. Nag at me too much, and I shall say something that I shall be sorry for after. Now you understand, don't you?"

"You are a peculiar young gentleman," said Miss Betterton. "I can't half make you out."

George is not prepared to offer any explanation, but he declares that on the return journey, as soon as the sun had gone down, and the insinuating twilight came, and lamps on board were lighted, he found his heart warming again with an affection for Miss Betterton. He tried to think of the compromising letter which he had read that morning, but even this document could not prevent him from admiring her. Whilst the other ladies on board were dusty and tired, with hair straight that once was wavy, and with temper fractious that once was equable, Miss Betterton looked as delightful and chattered away as good-temperedly as ever.

George went so far once as to stroke her wrist, but Miss Betterton, glancing at the silent Mervale, spoke to George reprovingly. Passing by Kew, singing commenced, and cheerful young gentlemen tipped their hats back and sang rollicking songs about meeting ladies on a 'bus, and about having too much to drink, and of being locked up, and of other diverting incidents; and young ladies closing their eyes sang, in a shrill stolid soprano, ballads of great emotion. When Miss Betterton's turn came, that young lady responded with alacrity (for it is not on board a steamboat that one may affect to excuse oneself; else is one incontinently passed over).

"I'm not in very good voice for singing," explained Miss Betterton to the circle, "but I can recite a piece if you like."

The silent Mervale moved forward, the better to hear, and there was a gallant murmur of encouragement.

"Is it long?" asked a lad.

"Depends," answered Miss Betterton, sharply, "what you call long. It is called 'The Spanish Maiden to her Lover,' and it's written in what is called blank verse."

"Fire away," said the lad.

Miss Betterton glanced at the admiring Mervale and rose. George, standing at the back out of sight, prepared to listen casually. It occurred to him, he tells me, at that moment, what a proud man he would be if he were to possess some day for a wife a lady so gifted in elocutionary gifts who could entertain company on early closing evenings in this refined and artistic manner.

"The Spanish Maiden to her Lover."

Miss Betlerton coughed and looked severely round until everyone had ceased talking. Then again the title.

"The Spanish Maiden to her Lover."

"Is that all?" asked the lad who had previously interrupted.

Miss Betterton killed him with a glance of reproof, and Mervale looked at him in a manner that caused the interrupting lad to take a serious complexion. Miss Betterton commenced her recitation in a high aggrieved tone—

"Alfonso, dearest, why do you remain
Away from everyone that holds you dear,
I, who desire your presence near to me,
Would—"

George could only restrain himself from rushing forward by holding on tightly to the white painted rail at the side of the steamer. The moment that the recitation was over, he forced his way insistently through the congratulating crowd and shook hands affectionately with the flushed artiste.

"I've thought of what I wanted to ask you this morning," he said softly.

"Really?"

"What I wanted to say was would you kindly go so far out of your way as to consent to become my wife?"

"Well," said Miss Belterton, calmly, "I don't know but what I might have done if you had asked me before. But down at Hampton Court Mr. Mervale was kind enough to make the same offer, and so— well, you're too late."

George Wraight, in relating to me this story, said that he is now engaged to Miss Oliffe, and wishes to remark in conclusion that what it seems to him to amount to is simply this. Some people {says George) are born lucky and some ain't. For his part, it seems to him that he belongs to the ain'ts.

A CONFLICT OF INTERESTS

"Captain Ballard", sitting opposite to me in the tea-shop in the Rue de Rivoli, sells me a copy of En Avant, and places the coins with some care in a small leather purse. I offer my St, James's, and "Captain"

Ballard reads an account of an interesting counterfeit coin case heard the previous morning at Clerkenwell Police-Court. She sighs when she reaches the finish of the report, and shakes her head and takes two more lumps of sugar.

"Ah," she says regretfully, "kerime, kerime, kerime! You can't stem it; you can't stop it; you can't retard it. On, on it goes, never ceasing, never ending. Ho, if only—"

I remark that there is presumably some attraction about the game.

"I never found it so," says "Captain" Ballard, with some tartness, smoothing her blue serge skirt. "It was always jolly 'ard work for me, that I do know. Before I found I'd got a soul I was as much in the thick of it as 'ere and there a one, and I think I'm entitled to speak a word or two on the subject. There was one affair I rec'lect—" She stopped herself. "It don't become any of us to brag onless we do it in a spirit of thenkfulness; but it does no 'arm to look back on them bad times, if only we can prove a warning to those dear bretheren and sisters who—"

When I manage to stop "Captain" Ballard's oration I ask her for particulars of the incident to which she has referred. "Captain" Ballard stirs the tea-pot, and leaning two elbows on the marble table, tells this tale.

On the day after Sir Benjamin bought the picture at Christie's Miss Ballard was engaged as lady's maid to his daughter. It was one of those strokes of luck which do not occur often (so Miss Ballard says) in one lifetime, and the excellent character produced by the new maid, together with her ability to speak colloquial French, considerably assisted her engagement. This shows the advantage of writing one's own testimonials.

"Now look here, my dear"—Sir Benjamin never spoke to the servants; his young daughter had full control over them—"I want them all warned that just for a day or so this most valuable and delightful Velasquez—I'm sure I can get more than I gave for it if I can only hit upon the right man—this picture will remain here; and I want everybody to keep their wits about them, Maggie, and there must be no loafers downstairs, or anything of that sort. See?"

"I understand, papa. This is Ballard, the new maid."

Sir Benjamin promptly turned his back upon Miss Ballard.

"Ask her whether she's got a sweet-heart?"

"No, indeed, Miss," said Miss Ballard with an indignant air. "I don't 'old with them for a single moment. I 've got something better to do than bother my head about a pack of grinning—"

"Because if she had," said Sir Benjamin to his daughter, "she would have had to understand that he mustn't come hanging around here. I hope they all clearly comprehend that."

"I think they ought, papa. We are always reminding them of it."

"Anything else, Miss."

"No, Ballard. Make the acquaintance of the others, and try to work as quietly as you can and avoid all disturbance."

"You trust me, Miss, for that. I don't suppose a more amiable person than me has ever been born on this earth; and as for quietness, why I don't think you'd find my equal. I'm sure the last place I had—it was in the country certainly, but that don't affect the argument—they couldn't find words to express what they thought of me."

"Tell her to go, Maggie," shouted Sir Benjamin hotly.

Miss Ballard, going downstairs, immediately made inquiries in regard to this stringent, and to her possibly inconvenient, rule in regard to followers.

"It's as much as your life is worth," said Cook regretfully, "to try it on. It's awk'ard I admit; but what can't be cured must be endured."

"It don't show much sympathy to'rds your fellow-creatures," remarked Miss Ballard. "I don't see any 'arm myself of one young man calling now and again. One isn't like a 'ole regiment."

"Your young man a army man, may I ask?" inquired Cook.

"No, indeed," said Miss Ballard proudly. "I do draw the line somewhere. My friend is in business on his own account and doing very well. He's been away on a—er—kind of 'oliday for some months—"

"Months?"

"Oh, well," said Miss Ballard, "if he likes to, why shouldn't he? He gets all his exes paid."

"I wonder whether I know his name?" said Cook.

"No," answered the new maid shortly, "you don't."

"You 've been in good families, I suppose, before this?"

"Good enough."

"There's many a worse one than this," remarked Cook. "The young mistress knows what's right and she knows what's wrong, and she will have what's right. Once she finds out you 're a-trying to play false with her, you get your month."

"I'm not trying to play false with her," declared Miss Ballard indignantly. "What do you mean by your 'ints?"

"I wasn't 'inting at all," answered Cook; "I was only just mentioning for your own private information out of the goodness of my 'eart, as you may say, that—"

"You keep the goodness of your 'eart to yourself, then," said the new maid definitely. "I can look after myself right enough."

"That's a good thing." Cook shivered with indignation. "I shouldn't think anyone else would want to do it for you. There's no need to fly all to pieces directly anyone 'appens to open their mouth; and whilst I think of it, perhaps you 'll kindly step out of my kitchen and not interfere with me in my work with your silly gossip. I 've got something else to do besides answering all your inquisitiveness."

"I'm going as fast as ever I can," said Miss Ballard, trembling, "and I bid you good afternoon."

"'Urry," said Cook.

When, later, a letter marked "Ergent" arrived addressed to Miss M. Ballard, Cook directed that it should be laid on the dresser so that Miss M. Ballard could find it if she liked. "Perhaps," added Cook, "it would learn her a lesson not to be so haughty in her manners. Civility," added Cook, with some severity, "civility becomes us all."

The house was late that night in retiring to rest. Several visitors called after dinner to see the Velasquez, and a South African person had offered Sir Benjamin a thousand pounds over and above the amount paid for the picture. At Sir Benjamin's express directions, his daughter locked the door very carefully, and placed the key on her bunch, and Miss Ballard took the key off' the bunch with the dexterity that practice brings. Her spirits revived under the prospect of success, and if it had not been so late she would have sent a telegram to Huntingdon Street, Hoxton.

"As it is," said Miss Ballard to herself brightly, "this little trick will have to be executed by Number One. Jim will be cross at being out of it, but Jim must put up with that. It 'll just show him that a woman's as capable if she only gets 'alf a chance as any amount of men. Jim has been just a leetle bit too 'igh and mighty once or twice of late, and though I didn't say an}'thing, I didn't like the way he threw his boot at me the other night. It wasn't what I call etiquette."

Miss Ballard crept downstairs very carefully. She was fully dressed ready to go out as soon as she had cut the canvas from the frame. She did not mind leaving her box behind, inasmuch as it contained only sufficient lumber to make it feel heavy. The way out into the area would be the most convenient exit.

"Steady does it," remarked Miss Ballard, softly. "Where's that key and where's that knife?"

There was a glimmer of gas in the library, and the Velasquez could just be seen dimly on the easel in the corner. Miss Ballard considered it wise not to turn up the gas, and taking the knife she cut the painting very closely at the edge of the old frame. The knife was very keen, and the job was nearly completed (the top only remained to be severed) when suddenly there was a grating noise of a window opening. She started back, and closing the knife, placed it in her pocket. The window opened slowly, and presently a man swung himself into the room. To Miss Ballard's terror, he went straight to the corner where she was.

"I'm very sorry," she pleaded in a whisper. "I'd no idea you were watching; I have n't done any particular 'arm."

The man turned his bull's-eye on her and did not speak.

"I can tell you 're a good sort, Sergeant," she went on, "from the kind look on your face." As a matter of fact, it was not possible to see his face; but it seemed a diplomatic thing to say. "I'm just going out of the 'ouse."

"Oh," he said, "just a-going are you? Not till I say you can go, young woman. You must kindly consider yourself my prisoner until I think fit to say otherwise. What is it? Case of going out to see your sweetheart, s'pose?"

"That was just it, Sergeant." The suggestion seemed to revive Miss Ballard's spirits. "You don't suppose for a moment, I hope, that it was anything else. I 've got what you may call a unspotted character, and it isn't likely I should want to go and rob the plate, or anything of that kind. If you don't mind, I 'll just step back to my room, thanking you for—"

"That's a nice old picture that," he said. The white shaft of light from his lantern waved round and settled on the Velasquez. "I'm a bit of a art lover myself, and—"

"Why," interrupted Miss Ballard, "you're not in uniform!"

"Well, I know that. Can't a 'tec dress in plain clothes?"

"But you don't, somehow, look like a 'tec."

"That's the cunning part of it," he said. "There ain't a better man at making up in all Scotland Yard than Robert Warkins."

"And are you engaged specially to look after this picture?"

"That is my identical business at the present time. I 've been waiting outside, but it's a bit parky there, and I don't know as I won't stay in 'ere for a bit. And if anybody comes in whilst I'm here, why—"

He took a neat little revolver from his trousers pocket.

"Well, you don't mind if I say good-night to you?" asked Miss Ballard with a regretful look at the picture. It was hard to have arrived so near to success, and then to have to leave.

"Not at all, my dear. Don't you go and lose your beauty sleep on my account. By-the-bye is there a new girl come to-day name of Ballard?"

"I rather think there is," said Miss Ballard, "but I haven't met her. I daresay I shall do sooner or later." Miss Ballard at the door seemed struck with a sudden thought and took her long white wrap from her neck. "Good night."

"Good night," he said. "Don't make a noise as you go upstairs."

"It's all right, Sergeant; I've got me boots off."

He turned, and, holding up his small bull's-eye lantern looked at the Velasquez and chuckled. Miss Ballard closed the door very quietly, and very softly crept up behind him. The white wrap went round thick and secure over his mouth, and was tied quickly; the revolver taken out of his pocket. The man, astounded, sank back for a moment into an arm-chair.

"Now look here. Sergeant: you just 'ark a—a bit to me."

She covered him with the revolver, and he made vain attempts to speak.

"You attempt to loosen that scarf that's over your mouth or you attempt to get out of that chair until I say 'Go,' and as sure as I'm a living woman you 'll never see Scotland Yard again. Understand that."

He looked at her appealingly but did not dare to move. A faint sound of suppressed grumbling came from his lips.

"Less noise there," said Miss Ballard, commandingly. "That's the worst of you detectives. You 're all jaw. Get up now and open that window. It isn't easy to see quite how to manage this business, but I'm going to do it. Open the window."

He complied with the order. He also gave a most appealing look to her, and raised his hand to undo the tight, well-tied knot at the back of his head.

"Ah," said Miss Ballard warningly, "would you? You do that again and pop goes this little pistol. Now I 'll just talk to you plainly, Sergeant. Sit down in that chair again."

He obeyed reluctantly, with one eye on his revolver, which she held steadily.

"I 'll tell you straightforwardly what I'm a-going to do. I'm a-going to pinch this painting and get away with it, whether you like it or not. If you don't like it, you can lump it!"

He smiled and would have moved his hands again towards the tight knot, only that the revolver jerked threateningly.

"I 've got the upper 'and of you now," she said, "and if you was the chiefest inspector ever born in Scotland Yard, you shouldn't interfere with me or stop me at the present point. This is serious business for me. Make so much as another move to untie that shawl, and your life won't be worth a bad threepenny bit."

With her left hand Miss Ballard cut the top line of the painting. Released, it slipped down on the floor. As it did so, the door opened behind her, and the muffled man in the chair made a swift rush for the window. The revolver dropped from the hands of the startled Miss Ballard and went off with a loud report.

"Now, then!" cried Miss Ballard; "you're doing what I told you not to. Why couldn't you keep quiet instead of—"

"You good, brave Ballard!" The voice of her young mistress made Miss Ballard turn. "You have stopped that dreadful burglar from stealing the beautiful picture. My father will never be able to thank you enough."

She was in her scarlet dressing-gown, and there was a look of mingled amazement and admiration in her eyes.

"What a smart, clever maid you are, Ballard. How did you have the courage to do it?"

"Well," said Miss Ballard modestly, "it had to be done, and I did it."

"But why are you wearing your bonnet?"

"I thought," explained Miss Ballard, "that I might have to chase him."

She went to the open window and looked down. The man had taken off the wrap, and, turning at the corner, he shook his fist at her.

"You silly Juggins," he shouted.

When the household had complimented Miss Ballard to its full and was returning again to rest after the commotion caused by the scare. Sir Benjamin elected to stay in the library for the rest of the night, and thanked his stars that the Velasquez was going away to its new purchaser the next day. Cook relented her harshness towards the new maid, and brought her the letter.

Miss Ballard read it—

Dear Martha,—A chum of mint is going to try to get in to-night. His name is Robert Warkins. Do all you can to help him.
Jim.

"I 'ope," said Cook graciously, "that we shall get on better than we begun. I'm a bit "asty in me temper, but if you 're 'ere for a bit longer I daresay we—"

"I 've had just enough of this shop," said Miss Ballard moodily; "I shall sling my 'ook at the very earliest opportunity."

"Captain" Ballard drinks up her tea (which is cold) and takes a lump of sugar, to be munched on her way home to the Rue Auber. She sighs a little regretfully.

"Ah well," she says, pulling her straw bonnet forward, "Glowry be it's all past and forgot now. There's a well-known 'ymn commencing—"

I am so afraid "Captain" Ballard is going to sing that I shake hands.

"Sinful days," says "Captain" Ballard as she grasps my hand, "Sinful days, but, my word, they was exciting."

A DETERMINED YOUNG PERSON

Jupiter took out one or two stars that required repairing, and placed them on a thick, grey cloud to be attended to in the morning. Juno, looking casually through the book of engagements—it was a large book—wrinkled her brow, and hummed softly and thoughtfully to herself.

"That's enough of it," said Jupiter, crossly; "I know that tune."

"What were you thinking of?" asked Mercury, respectfully. Mercury had just seen that the mail trains were safely dispatched, and was keeping one eye on the railway system generally.

"I was thinking that it wouldn't be a bad plan," said Juno, "if it could be arranged, for no girl to be married more than once. Then we should get these figures something like right."

Jupiter snorted, and moved his lips silently as one who does not care to trust himself to speech. Mercury coughed, and remarked, diplomatically, that, of course, there was something in the idea, but—

"Well," said Juno. "But what?"

"I should like to tell a tale," said Mercury.

And he did.

Mr. Frank Northfleet was brushing his silk hat in his office in a state of great good spirits. He had changed into evening dress at the office of the Rorty Well Mining Company, and was going by Underground, Sloane Square way, to dinner.

"After dinner," said Mr. Frank Northfleet, "I shall go upstairs and I shall get her aunt to play, and, whilst the aunt is playing, I shall say, 'Kate, dear, I want to ask you to be my wife. I am earning—'"

There was a knock at the door—the clerks had gone—and Mr. Northfleet went to open it.

"Name of Northfleet," said the telegraph boy.

"Thank you, my boy." Mr. Northfleet took the telegram. He was slightly anxious at the prospect of to-night's essay, and he thought it would be wise to propitiate the gods by being generous. "Just off home?"

"Rather," said the boy. "I shall be late, too. Going to the theatre."

"Good," said Mr. Northfleet. "Here's half-a-crown to pay for your seat."

"This," said the telegraph boy, as he took the coin and placed it with much good humour in his eye, "is a bit of all right."

Mr. Frank Northfleet opened the envelope.

Northfleet,
Lothbury
London.

"Mine partly flooded. Grierson gone. Come out.—Blenkinsop."

The young Secretary sat down in the chair and gasped. Half unconsciously he pulled off his dress tie. Then he rose and hurried to the telephone. The Chairman of the Company was abroad, and the Directors were quite useless. He felt that the responsibility for action rested with him alone.

"Hullo there."

"Hullo you."

"Is that Mr. Winstanley?"

"Yes."

"Can you go out by to-morrow morning's ship to our mines? There's trouble there. The Scot goes to-morrow."

A sound of whistling at the other end.

"I thought the water was going into the Rocky Gorge Mines. It's gone your way instead, then?"

"That's about it, Winstanley. Can you go?"

"Only too pleased. Two thousand pounds."

"Two thousand what?"

"That's my fee."

Argument had no effect in reducing this unprepossessing figure. Northfleet knew that he had no authority to expend this sum.

"Then I suppose I must go myself," said Northfleet with a sigh.

"Right you are. Good-night. You know where to find me if you change your mind. Russell Square."

Mr. Northfleet was shown into the drawing-room in Cheyne Gardens, and was welcomed by Mrs. Locke Hardinge and by Mrs. Locke Hardinge's mother. She was a very charming young person, Mrs. Hardinge; none the less charming for being just now very much in love. Mr. Frank Northfleet stated the case as briefly as possible.

"Mamma dear," said young Mrs. Hardinge, with some hurry. "Will you just see if everything is ready in the dining-room? You know what servants are."

She turned to Northfleet as soon as the obedient parent had disappeared.

"You are not really going, Mr. Northfleet?"

"Unfortunately I am. If I go from Waterloo to-night, I shall be able to buy a few things at Southampton to-morrow morning before I get on board to-morrow. I'm not like this expensive man, Winstanley; I want a few moments' notice."

"I'm—I'm very sorry you are going."

"So am I. As a fact"—he took her hand—"I was going to ask you to-night to be my wife."

She caught her breath for a moment, and did not answer.

"And if you care for me," went on Northfleet, "I shan't so much mind going. Absence will only make my heart grow fonder."

"Yes," she said, thoughtfully, "fonder of somebody in South Africa. Look here, Mr. Northfleet, I had money in the Rocky Gorge Mines, and that's all right now. I'll let you have the two thousand."

He did not hesitate for a moment.

"I couldn't take it, dear. It's very good of you, but—"

"I think you are very silly," she said, decidedly.

"Silly, perhaps," he said, "but not mean. I could not possibly be under so great an obligation to you, dear girl."

"Am I your dear girl?"

"Why, I hope so."

"But I may not be when you return. Do you happen to know, sir, how old I am now?"

"You are old enough to make me a dear, delightful—"

"Question, question. Do you know how old I am? I am twenty-four." Mr. Northfleet affected extreme surprise at the magnitude of the figure. "And when you return I shall be twenty-seven, and twenty-seven is getting on for thirty, and you will find some—some diamond merchant's daughter, or whatever the product of the country is, and—Don't go, I can so easily spare the money."

"I should feel, dearest love," said Frank Northfleet, "that I was doing a dishonourable thing, and you must please let me have my own way. My mind is quite made up. But I confess I wish I hadn't to go."

Mr. Frank Northfleet was at Waterloo Station at half-past nine that evening. It had been hard work to say good-bye to her, but they had managed to have a good long talk, and although he might be away for a couple of years, they were going to correspond very frequently. He took his ticket, and put his portmanteau in a first smoking.

"It wants ten minutes," said the guard. "What might be your name, sir, may I ask?"

"It might be, and indeed is, Northfleet."

"Would you mind stepping this way, please? Someone wants to see you."

A veiled Sister of Mercy! She was standing in the shadow of the bridge on the opposite side of the platform. She took Frank Northfleet by the hand.

"Zere is no time to loose," she said, in queer broken English. "Do not, if you please, say a single word."

"Well, but—"

"Listen to me, if you please." She led him a little aside.

"It is all goontrived ver' well, and the stolen bonds haf been sold."

"Oh," said Frank Northfleet, with a puzzled air. "That's a very good thing."

"We all leaf England at once, but you, of course, remain here; is it not so?"

"Naturally," he said.

It occurred to Mr. Northfleet that this would be a diverting incident for him to relate (with a little exaggeration) on the Scot to his fellow-voyagers. It also occurred to him that he would make the Sister of Mercy extremely young and handsome (which she was not, for there were lines of age on her face).

"Zey all send their best regards," continued the Sister of Mercy, "and zey hope you will be quite happy."

"Oh, I shall he all right," said Mr. Northfleot, laughingly. "Tell them not to worry about me."

"And you vill never forget me?"

"Never; I give you my word of that. But do you know somehow I almost forget the circumstances. It was rather—rather a startling affair, wasn't it?"

"It was gapitally managed," said the mysterious Sister of Mercy. "For my part I haf heen engaged in so excellent an affair never in all my life. I hope you von't spoil it."

"And the detectives?" Mr. Northfleet felt that it would make the incident more interesting if he could only get at the details, "Is there no fear from New Scotland Yard?"

"Police know nozzing," she said, with much exultation. "It has all been managed so admirable. Yoseph— you remember Yoseph?"

"I am not likely to forget Joseph," said Mr. Northfleet, acutely.

"He is abroad to America gone."

"That's a good thing. But I have a fearful memory, as you know—"

"You vas allevays forgetting somethings."

"Well," asked Northfleet, ingeniously, "where did the robbery take place?"

"Oh, you foony fellow," said the Sister of Mercy. "As if you didn't know quite well. You had no hand in it; but, of course, there is your share to gonsider."

"Of course."

"If you never see me again you will not forget me, eh?"

The question was put with some anxiety.

"It is not likely."

There was no harm in being polite to so old a woman.

"And now zere is but one zing to be done."

She felt in the bosom of her dress and looked anxiously at the clock.

"Oh," said Northfleet. "It's not really finished yet, then."

"Ah," said the Sister of Mercy, "allevays the merry one of the party. You like my disguise, eh?"

She had a small canvas bag in her hands.

"Oh, I think it capital," said Frank Northfleet, with an amused air. "You look exceedingly well in it; but I must take my seat in the train."

"First," she handed him the bag, "here is your share. Two thousand fife hundred pounds in notes. Goo'-bye."

She shook hands, turned hastily, and hurried away.

"Two thousand five hundred pounds," repeated Northfield, mechanically.

"You've dropped something, sir," said the guard. He held it up to the light. "As nice a 'undred-pound note as anyone might wish to see. You'd better take your seat, sir."

"Well, but—but there's some extraordinary blunder. This money is not mine!"

"I shall be 'appy," said the guard, politely, "to blew as much of it, sir, as you like to leave me in your will. There's nothing like possession in these matters."

"Can you stop that woman?"

"There's no stopping a woman, sir," said the guard, with the manner of one who knows the sex. "She's 'ooked it. Jump in, sir."

It was so obviously an act of Providence that it really seemed impious to hesitate further.

"I think I'd better not," cried Frank Northfleet. "Take my portmanteau out; I'm not going. Russell Square, cabman."

It was rather late that evening when Mrs. Locke Hardinge looked into the glass in her bedroom. The washing of her pretty face and the hard rubbeeng had not only removed the make-up, but had given to her cheeks—she had an excellent cheek—a glow which rouge, however well intentioned, never really attains. Her cheque-book was open on the dressing-table. On the bed lay the demure cap and white bands and gown of a Sister of Mercy.

"The trouble," said Mrs. Locke Hardinge, as she looked at the counterfoil of the cheque that she had that evening written, "the trouble that there is in this world to get married a second time and to find someone to cash a cheque for you after banking hours is—well, something tremendous."

Mercury, as he finished his story, moistened his lips with a passing shower.

"Now," he said, "what are you to do when there are such determined young women as that to deal with?"

Juno thought. She looked at Jupiter (who was asleep), and she remembered her Lemprière, and the anecdotes of her own early days contained therein.

"Ah, well," she said, tolerantly; "I suppose girls will be girls all the world over, especially young widows."

FRECKLES

Usually the 6.32 p.m. from London stopped in a casual way at the small wooden station whose name was set out in giant letters of whitened pebbles on the bank; and the engine having sneezed while one or two passengers alighted, and the guard having told the office-boy that if he received any more cheek he would report the office-boy to the Superintendent, the train went on to pursue its journey into the heart of Kent. A July evening found commotion on the narrow platform which a sun had been baking all day, so that the shoes of the waiting villagers left imprints on its tarred and gravelled surface; the office-boy, big with importance and glad to show authority in the presence of a long-limbed, freckled-faced girl who stood back near to the bed of geraniums, ordered them to stand back and go higher up and to come lower down, all in the way of a bustling dog controlling a flock of sheep.

"All with no tickets," shouted the office-boy presently, as the train came in sight far away on the straight lines, "get off of the platform."

"We 're expectin' of somebody," urged one or two of the elders. The freckled-faced girl prepared to leave.

"You can stop where y' are," whispered the office-boy to her. She nodded and came back. "All the rest get down there by the signal-box and wait," he ordered authoritatively.

They obeyed, and made a lump of patient heads near to the level crossing as the oncoming engine whistled at them and drew the train up to a halt. Three or four London children who had had their heads out of the window turned the brass handles and jumped out on the platform. Each bore a label, tied around the neck, and the one boy of the party was addressed to Mrs. Naylor, of Rose Cottage. The long-limbed girl stepped forward to him.

"You want Mrs. Naylor, don't ye?" she asked shyly.

"Wha's that to do with you?" demanded the short boy from London. He had a sharp, acute face, with his hair brought down well over his forehead; his collar was clean, but worn at the edges.

"She's down this way."

"Dessay I can find her," said the short boy curtly, "without you puitin' your spoke in."

"Let me carry your parcel for ye."

"Look 'ere," said the boy, with truculence, "when you 're wanted you shall be sent for. Meanwhile, keep yourself to yourself, and don't you interfere with me. Unnerstand that, if you please."

The train went on, and the children, giving up their tickets to the office-boy, offered themselves and their labels to the consideration of women waiting for them. A hard-faced middle-aged woman took the short boy, and, catching his hand sharply, took him over the level crossing without a word; the long-limbed girl following at a space of a few yards. They walked across the station yard with other women and children to the main road, where they separated.

"You seem to have a rare fund of lively conversation, you country people," remarked the boy satirically, as they went down the dusty road. "Don't you get tired sometimes of talkin' so much?"

"Less noise from you," said the hard-faced woman, "if you please."

"Your name Naylor?" asked the boy.

"Mrs. Naylor," she admitted.

"Mine's Sizzle," he said proudly. "Sizzle Aub'ron Tabor. Lay you don't get eristocratic nimes like Sizzle down ere in this Gaud-forsaken place."

"We have what chrissen names we like," replied the woman tartly.

"What's yours?"

"My chrissen name is Ruth. My 'usban's name is Saul. Both," added Mrs. Naylor, showing in her turn something of conceit, "both took straight from the Bible."

"Well, I'm 'anged!" remarked the boy.

"And you'll have to behave yourself," went on Mrs. Naylor inconsequently, "the fortnight you 're stayin' down 'ere; and you let me find you up to any of your London tricks, and I 'll punish you jest the same as if you was me own boy."

"How many kids you got?" asked Master Cecil Tabor.

"'Eaven," said Mrs. Naylor, with something of a catch in her voice, "'Eaven 'an't blessed us with no children. There's only the two of us, Saul and me."

"You 're a juggins," remarked the boy, "to worry about that. There's plenty of youngsters up in Red Cross Street, where I come from. I reckon anyone could buy as many as they liked there for about three a penny."

"This is where we live," said Mrs. Naylor. "Come around 'ere to the back. Goo'-night, Sarerann." The girl responded.

"Why not go in the front door?" asked the boy.

"Because it ain't Sunday," she replied curtly. "Give your shoes a brush with this bass-broom."

The boy looked back at the roadway as the long-limbed girl passed, and noticed that she went on towards the next cottage, the garden of which was separated from that of Rose Cottage by a wooden barred fence. He imitated the warning sound of an approaching bicycle, and was pleased to see that the girl started affrightedly. In the garden someone who appeared to be a gentleman of colour was washing himself at a basin stood upon a wicker-bottomed chair, and he looked up, his grimy face covered with soapsuds, as the two came into view.

"Wha' cheer, Rewth," he said, nibbeeng the water from his eyes. "You 've found 'm then?"

"Can't you see I have," she replied tartly. "Get rid some cf that coal-dust and come in to your tea."

"'Aving a bit of a sluice down, ole man?" asked Master Tabor familiarly.

"Jest gettin' one or two coatin's off," replied Mr. Naylor. "Jiggered if I don't sometimes wish I was a miller 'stead of being in the mucky coal business."

"It makes you a bit dark-complexioned," agreed the boy. "You ought to treat yourself to a powder-puff."

Mr. Naylor had dipped his face again into the basin of soap-water, but on hearing this he threw his head back and roared cheerfully, repeating the last words of the boy's remark with great enjoyment. He came into the kitchen presently with his eyes still black and a dusky look about the rest of his face, and when his wife told him (not, it seemed, for the first time) that his hands were a disgrace to the village, he took the reproach good-temperedly. The three sat down at the white-clothed table to a bread-and-butter tea with green young lettuces tearful at having been plunged into water, and a home-made cake that the boy eyed acutely.

"A pretty character you are," said Mrs. Naylor bitterly, "to 'elp me look after this boy for a 'ole fortnight. Why, to look at you, anyone would think you were a—"

"Say grace, Rewth."

"For what we are 'bout receive Lord make us truly thankful," said Mrs. Naylor, bowing her head. "A low tramp!" she added, looking up.

"What made you marry him?" asked the boy from his side of the table.

"There!" she said with melancholy triumph, "even the boy asks that question. It's a puzzle to everyone, young and old, 'igh and low, rich and—"

"I suppose," said the boy, eating with great appetite, "it was only because you couldn't get no one else to."

"Jigger me!" roared Mr. Naylor with great delight, "if the boy ain't hit the nayul right on the head."

"And I 'll hit him there too," said the woman sharply, "if he talks with his mouth full. Pull up your chair closer, me lad, and behave, and leave off sniffin'."

There seemed at first some probability that the advent of Master Cecil Tabor would increase the number of domestic jars at Rose Cottage, but the fact appeared to be that Mrs. Naylor had always reached a high standard of acerbity, and any change that she made could only be in the direction of amiability. Indeed, later in the evening, when the boy from the Borough, on being ordered to bed, obtained a respite by proceeding to give imitations of music-hall favourites whom he had seen at the South London Palace, he succeeded in arousing a smile from Mrs. Naylor that had been dormant so long that it seemed rather confused and awkward, but was presently followed by other smiles of more assurance. Feeling, later on, that this show of interest was undignified, she gave the boy a good shake and took him up to his small bed-room, where she delivered from the landing, as he undressed, a brief address on the sin of going to theatres, pointing out that these bordered the way to destruction, besides costing money. The boy listened to her for some time, and then, being tired, assured her that she knew nothing of what she was talking, and turning his tired young head on the pillow, went instantly to sleep. Mrs. Naylor walked downstairs and upbraided her husband for not having brought home his cash to be locked up in the usual way.

The boy was taking a first survey of the back garden the next morning, in order to ascertain the possibilities for mischief, when a head appeared over the wooden fence—a head that at this early hour of the day was so fiercely studded with curling-pins that it looked at first sight as though the young woman wore a silver helmet. She coughed, and the boy started from the white currant-bush to which he had been applying himself.

"'Ello!" he said, regaining his composure, "Freckles!"

"My name ain't Freckles," said the girl, "it's Sarerann Francis."

"Your nime's Freckles," he retorted. "Don't you get in the 'abit of conterdictin'. My name's Sizzle Aub'ron."

"I think I shall call you Suet Puddin'," she said shyly. "You 're very white about the face."

"I can see what's the matter with you," remarked the boy threateningly, "you want your 'ead punched. Stay where you are, and in about two twos—"

"Don't hit me," begged Freckles, bobbeeng down on her side of the fence. "I don't like being hit."

"What's my nime, then?" asked the boy threateningly.

"Sizzle something."

"Sizzle Auberon Tabor." The shrinking girl repeated it carefully. "Ah!" said the London boy, "don't you ferget it, mind, or else you 'll be sorry you was ever born."

"Come out and have game cricket presently, when I 've finished 'elping mother with the 'ousework," suggested the young woman.

"Dem fine 'and at cricket, you."

"I can bowl round-arm," she said. "and chance it. 'Ev you ever played?"

"Been at it all me life," said the boy, with some want of exactness. "I'm the chempion in our street. We get a jacket and fold it up against the wall, and we make a ball out of anything we can get 'old of, and a bit of wood for a bat, and—

"Sarerann!" called a voice. "Come 'ere this minute, you good-fer-nothing young 'ussy, you!"

"Ten o'clock," whispered Freckles, preparing to go.

"P'raps I shall be there and p'raps I shan't."

As a matter of fact, the boy found himself turned out of the cottage after breakfast, Mr. Naylor having started on a round from his coal depôt with a wagon loaded with fat sacks of coal, and Mrs. Naylor, first tying a handkerchief fiercely around her head, and enveloping herself in a brown holland cover, threw herself with remarkable energy into the work of giving the place a tidy up, which appeared to consist in taking every spotless article laboriously from its place, dusting it, rubbeeng it, breathing on it and rubbeeng it again, and eventually returning it to its place in its former immaculate condition. To escape being treated in like manner, the boy went out into the roadway, and discovered presently, to his great annoyance, near a dry ditch into which he slipped, the reason why stinging nettles are so called. He was kicking the nettles and swearing at them resentfully, when a stump fell near him, followed by three more, followed also by a ball. Picking these up, he saw Freckles pointing with one long arm down the road, and he obeyed by carrying them in the direction indicated. There he found a triangle of grass with a barn at the base, which bore posters of a long-departed circus. Freckles appearing, the wickets were pitched, and Freckles said, "Dolly I first innings"; but the boy shouted, "Bags I first go!" and, seizing the bat, declared that in Red Cross Street, Borough, and in other places in London where the national game was played, men always batted first, and girls had to bowl. Anxious to comply with the rulings of town. Freckles took the ball and sent down a round-armer that missed the boy's bat and hit his wicket; but he declined to give up the bat on the ground that the first ball was always given "for love," and was never taken seriously. He found many other ingenious excuses afterwards for not going out, with the result that Freckles had to do most of the running in her awkward long-legged way. The London girls who had arrived with him went by in charge of one of the villagers, and he was about to holloa to them when Freckles begged him not to speak to them, and he consented, with the proviso that she should acknowledge that he could beat her at cricket—a wholly unfounded claim, to which she at once gave her cordial consent.

"What's your father work at for a livin'?" she asked, as they walked back for dinner.

"He don't work at all," replied the boy, glancing at her aggressively. "You mind yer own business, Freckles."

"Is he independent?"

"Yes."

"Live at home?"

"No he don't," snapped the boy. "He's put away at Wormwood Scrubbs jest now, if you must know."

"Why don't you and your mother go with him?"

The boy looked at her curiously, as though to ascertain whether her attitude was one of ignorance or whether she was only assuming this as a cloak for impudence. He appeared satisfied.

"Silly kid!" he said disdainfully.

The other days of the first week saw him increasing in the favour of his hosts and in the admiration of Freckles. His alertness, his quaint effrontery, his comic songs, his amazing coolness—all these things were new to the couple in whose cottage he was living; when it was found that they were backed up, after a few days, by unexpected little touches of affection, then even Mrs. Naylor gave up her attitude of reproach, and her voice softened when she spoke of him. And when Mr. Naylor was engaged in the laborious work of making up his accounts in the evening and checking his cash the boy was of real use, for he could tell how much five hundredweight at twenty-five shillings a ton came to before Mr. Naylor had written the figures on the slate. Sunday came, and he was conveyed, much against his wish, to the Congregational Chapel, where he showed some signs of restlessness during the prayers, and murmured, "Time, time!" under his breath; but his interest awoke when Freckles and other muslin-dressed young women of the parish, up in the gallery near the harmonium, commenced to sing. Later in the day he so far unbent as to make a defiant offer to Freckles across the wooden fence to accompany her to evening service, and Freckles, walking with him into chapel that evening, knew the joy of pride.

Because everything in this world has an end, Cecil Auberon Tabor's holiday finished, and the office-boy at the station was perhaps the only person in the village who was glad of this. Mrs. Naylor baked vigorously all through the day that the boy might have something to eat on his two hours' journey to London ("He must keep body and soul together," said Mrs. Naylor), and was thus enabled to load him up with meat pasties and cake in sufficient quantity to have kept the whole party of child visitors for a week. To her great regret, Freckles was unable to see him off at the station: the absence of her mother with a married daughter Linton way obliged her to remain in charge of her house, but the London boy kissed her, and said that likely as not they might run up against each other again. Freckles was only able to wave a tearful farewell as the train rushed Londonwards with brown faces of excited children out of the window. Mr. Naylor from the coal-wharf also sent up an adieu that might have been shouted by a fog-horn.

"Saul!" cried Mrs. Naylor that evening.

"Now begin again," answered Mr. Naylor, from his wash-hand stand.

"Come 'ere this minute! Come at once! We 've been robbed! There's been burglars! Oh, Saul, we 're ruined!"

"You're makin' a lot o' fuss 'bout nothin' at all, I expect," remarked Mr. Naylor, as he came in leisurely.

"That fi'-pun note that you locked up safe in the tea-caddy last night is gone!"

"Well I'm jiggered!" exclaimed Mr. Naylor. The two stood looking blankly at the caddy "Sims almost," said Mr. Naylor hesitatingly, "as though our—your London boy must have been and gone and took it."

"Saul," replied Mrs. Naylor, "you was a fool when I knew ye first, and a fool you 'll be till the end of the world. I'd trust that dear boy with untold gold."

"But this was a fi'-pun note," urged Mr. Naylor, thinking he had detected a flaw in the premises.

"I'm ashamed of you. Paul, for even dreamin' of such a thing."

"Any way," said Mr. Naylor, "it's gone."

"Yes," admitted Mrs. Naylor, "it's clean gone. We 'd better send for young 'Obman."

Young Mr. Hobman arriving, took off his peaked cap with its little rampant silvered horse and loosened his waist-belt, and said at the outset that he should have been sent for earlier. When the unreasonableness of this remark was pointed out, P.C. Hobman waved the protests aside and remarked that he had not belonged to the Kent County Constabulary for eighteen months without knowing something of the Law, and if this did not mean a case for the Assizes why then he would eat his walking-stick. Mrs. Naylor ventured to submit that it was necessary, before having a case at the Assizes, first to catch a prisoner, and P.C. Hobman, admitting the force of this rather grudgingly, applied himself to the work of investigation. He searched the back garden for footprints, and Freckles, who had heard all the foregoing talk, watched him from the fence nervously.

"You 've had a bit of a boy from London staying with you," said P.C. Hobman presently. The two nodded. "Then," said the Constable, "it's him what's took it!"

"You're a darned young idiot," burst out Mrs. Naylor, with vehemence.

"That's as may be," said P.C. Hobman equably. "But, anyhow, I 'll borr' a trap and drive over and see our Instructin' Constable, and we 'll see what steps ought to be took."

"Better be half go and look after them gipsies," suggested Mrs. Naylor wildly. "Them's the characters what do all this sort of thieving."

Freckles, from the fence, gave a sigh of relief that was but temporary.

"The boy took it," said P.C. Hobman doggedly. "The gipsies cleared off two days ago. I 'll trot up to London Bridge by the parley in the momin' and we 'll nab him in rather less than no time."

"Hi!" said a voice from the other side of the wooden fence.

"Did you call, Sarerann?"

"Yes," said the girl, with a white face. "I can save you the trouble of sending up to London. I took your fi'-pun note."

"And what have you done with it, you bad, wicked, good-for—"

"Burnt it," said Freckles.

"Whatever for?"

"For fun," said Freckles.

"Call your mother this minute."

"She won't be home to-night," said Freckles calmly. "There's a new baby at sister Judith's at Linton."

"My girl," said P.C. Hobman, "I shall most likely have to cart you into Maidstone first thing in the mornin'."

"1 don't care," said Freckles, with a nervous effort at impudence. "I don't of'en get an outing."

"I ought to take you to-night."

"I 'll look sharp after her to-night," said Mrs. Naylor, "whilst you go and see your Instructing Constable about it. And I 'll give her such a talkin' to—"

Poor Freckles, under lock and key in the room that had been occupied by the boy from London, had to listen to Mrs. Naylor's hard, reproachful voice for many hours that night—the while Mr. Naylor slept peaceably. She took all the reproofs without sign of emotion, until Mrs. Naylor pictured the contempt and indignation of the new baby nephew at Linton. In the morning she prepared stolidly for the arrival of the constable. She was looking out of the window, ready dressed for the journey to Maidstone, when a whistle clipped her attention.

"Hullo!" said the office-boy. "In the wrong 'ouse, ain't you?"

"Shall be in a wronger one soon," said Freckles ruefully.

"Got a parcel for Mrs. Naylor," called the boy. "Tell her to 'urry down and sign for it. I must get back sharply to my monthly abstract."

The signature "R. Naylor" being written in the office-boy's book, Mrs. Naylor took the clumsily tied little parcel. It was really more like an amateur envelope than a parcel, and it contained a letter—

I took this away by mistake in the hurry, and I send it back with comps. I am very sorry. Please forgive me. I am going to be a better boy.

Yours truly,
Cecil Auberon Tabor.

Don't tell Freckles.

The five-pound note was inside.

"Sarerann," said Mrs. Naylor solemnly, "when he grows up, your new little nephew will be as proud as proud o' you."

A QUESTION OF POLICY

The Climax Tea-Rooms were doing an excellent trade—the hour being six o'clock, p.m.—and young Mrs. Bell, the proprietress, bustled up and down between the two rows of oblong marble tables, hurrying the two moon-faced young women who assisted her, temporising with waiting customers, and welcoming new arrivals. The window facing East India Dock Road bore strips of paper plastered upon it, giving the suggestion that it had been in a fight and had got rather the worst of it, closer inspection proved that these bore enticing notices. "A Fourpenny Tea for Twopence! Good Manners and Good Food! We Invite a Trial!" Waiting customers found the journals which are still called comic to inspect; others, who had been served, propped an evening paper against their metal teapot to read an alluring inquest case, the while they blew at the contents of their cup and sipped noisily. A clean-shaven brown-faced man, with an undecided chin, came in between the swing-doors and sat cautiously on a vacant seat near the window. He concealed himself in ambush behind a Star.

"Good evening, Sir!" said young Mrs. Bell. "Lovely weather for the time of the year, isn't it?" Mrs. Bell held a plate of thick toast which she was conveying to another customer. "Cup of tea? Anything else?"

"Yes," said the clean-shaven man in a hoarse whisper.

"What like, Sir?"

"You!" he said, glancing suddenly over the edge of the Star.

"Robert!" she exclaimed. The toast slipped from the plate to the floor. "What—what's made you come back?"

"Fact of the matter is—" he began

"'Ush!" she said with great concern. She stooped to pick up the pieces of toast.

"All right," he said obediently. "I'll 'ush, then, Louiser."

The two assistants came up to him at intervals when the stress of customers relaxed, and brought newspapers. Mrs. Bell, trembling, glanced frequently in his direction, and the cups and saucers that she handled rattled and chinked. The elder round-faced assistant stood by his table and, sweeping imaginary crumbs from it, inspected him curiously.

"Seafarin' gentleman?" she asked

"Pardon?"

"I say," repeated the waitress, "are you a seafaring"—she glanced at his hands—"person?"

"To a certain extent," he said with reserve, "I am."

"Must be very nice and open to be sailin' on the ocean wave. What I mean is, it can't be nearly so stuffy, you see, as being cooped up in a place like this with the gas going all day. The sea, now, must be so different."

"It 's got its drawbacks," said the man.

"After all, though." remarked the waitress, "I expect you 're glad to get back to London again." She smiled at him. "Nice to get back, you see, to your wife."

"WHAT?" roared the man.

"Ain't you married? " she asked.

"Look 'ere." he said with asperity. "D'ye know what you are talkin' about?"

"Keroline!" called her mistress from place; the clatter and rattle and bang of the counter.

"Yes'm."

"Come 'ere this instant, and help wash up."

When the tea-rooms were nearly free of patrons, Mrs. Bell came slowly down the gangway to the customer. He was still there, behind the evening paper, and she spoke to him in a low voice as she looked out at East India Dock Road and at the people hurrying homeward to Bow. The two young assistants were clearing off traces of the struggle that had just taken traffic outside helped to prevent the conversation from being heard.

"Whatever possessed you?" demanded Mrs. Bell. "If there's anything foolish to be done, you must he at it."

"Why," he expostulated, "ain't I your 'usband? After all—"

"I told you I'd send for you when it was safe for you to come back. And 'ere you come blunderin' into the place—"

"I come in like a gentleman."

"And you'd better go out like one," she said. "Sooner you get away from here the better."

"Better for who?"

"Better for you," she said meaningly; "better for everybody."

"I like the way you talk," said Mr. Bell with satire. "Anybody'd think I hadn't any business 'ere."

"More you have n't. This is my business. I bought it with the money as I wrote and told you that come to me over your insurance policy. When I'm ready to pay it back, I'll let you know. At present you 're supposed to be dead."

"Supposed to be," he admitted: "But," he added with spirit, "I ain't."

"You 'll look silly if you come to life now, Robert," said his wife.

"I shall look sillier if I don't. How long d' you think I'm going to keep playin' in this blooming farce, Louiser?" he asked, tapping at the marble table.

"Leave off knockin' that table, and listen to me. Do you know what 'll 'appen if you 're recognised?"

"Bah!" said Mr. Bell uneasily. "Who'd recognise me without me beard and mestache? Who'd be likely to come all the way from Rotherhithe and—"

"Once you're recognised," said Mrs. Bell solemnly, "you'll find yourself in the 'ands of the law. And d'you know what the law 'll say to you? I 've made it my business to find out, Robert. For pretendin' to be dead, and wrong information being sent home by others to your widow, and her thereby getting a matter of two 'undred pounds out of an insurance company, the penalty is—"

She turned, and bent down to whisper.

Go on with you!" said Mr. Bell with great concern. "Who's been filling your silly young 'ead with that nonsense? The lor can see a joke as well as anyone. Besides, it wasn't my fault that they thought I was done for."

"If you don't believe me, ask someone else. 'Ere's a sergeant going along outside now. Shall I call him in, and—?"

"Don't you go being a stupid young stupid," begged Mr. Bell, wiping his forehead with a scarlet handkerchief. "Can't you see that you'd get into trouble as well?"

"Pardon me," she said. "I simply acted on the letter and the certificate what come to me. And if you think I'm going to pay back the two 'undred this week just for the sake of you—"

"Yes, but— Look 'ere, Louiser. Try to unnerstand. You, being a fond and, I may say, affectionate wife, you naturally want your husband to be here with you and give a 'and with business Don't you now?"

"I can manage the shop by meself," said Mrs. Bell.

"Granted, granted," he said anxiously. "A better business-woman never lived. All the same, you naturally want me to stay on and make meself generally useful."

"Do I, indeed?"

"As you very properly argue, a wife has got a perfect right to expect that her husband shall make his home under the same roof as her, and not to go voyaging about on a cargo-vessel that doesn't keep in the same position for two seconds together. And, mind you, I think you 're right."

"I'm gettin' along," declared Mrs. Bell, "very well as I am, Robert, and I don't want no interference either from you or anyone else. I'm a widow woman with a character to keep up in Poplar, and—"

"How can you talk like that when I'm your lorful married husband sitting 'ere and drinkin' cold coffee?"

"Ah!" said Mrs. Bell with a sigh, "it'd be different, of course, if you was still alive."

"I'm as live as ever I was."

"You dare to go and tell that to the insurance company!"

There was a pause. Mr. Bell rose, found his new bowler hat, and first punched a dent in it and then punched out the dent.

"For aggravatingness," he siiid strenuously, "for want of logic, and for general wrong-'eadedness, commend me to a woman."

"Good evening, Sir," she said loudly as she opened the door for him, "and thank you!"

Mr. Robert Bell walked home to his lodging in Pekin Street, Poplar, a moody and a solitary man. He had been back in England but twenty-four hours, and it seemed to him that although life on a sailing-vessel had many grievous drawbacks, a sailing-vessel was ahead of London for comfort. There, at any rate, he had always been able to console himself with the thought of a cordial welcome at some distant date; by endeavouring to anticipate that joy he had, it appeared, only succeeded in giving it indefinite postponement He had assumed the name of Merriweather on his return, and this name he had given to his new landlady, together with erroneous information to the effect that he had relatives in the neighbourhood whose address he had forgotten.

"I 've found 'em!" said his landlady exultantly, as he stumbled into the narrow, dimly lighted passage. She turned up the little oil-lamp standing on the bracket, and the oil-lamp, annoyed, began to smoke furiously. "I 've found 'em, Mr, Merriweather, and glad enough I am to have been of some service to you." She was a vivacious old lady in a beaded cap, with a lively knowledge of the affairs of other people, and just now keenly interested in the new occupant of her bed-sitting-room. "And you mustn't thank me, because I'm only too pleased to bring friends and relatives together."

"Now what are you cacklin' about, Ma'am?" he asked politely.

"Ah," replied the old lady cheerfully, "you 'll soon know. We shan't be long now. It 'll be as good as a play to see you two meet." She wept and rubbed her eyes. "People may say what they like, but there's nothing in all this wide world to be compared to two lovin' 'earts."

"Let me have my supper," he said patiently, "and then leave me be. I want to have a smoke and a think."

"You won't do much thinking," remarked the landlady knowingly, "when you 'ear the news I 've got for you. You said your name was Merriweather, didn't you?"

"I don't deny it."

"And you said you'd got friends near 'ere—you'd forgot the address."

"I might have let fall a casual remark," said Mr. Bell carefully, as he held the handle of his door, "or statement to that effect. Whatever I said I 'll slick to."

"I knew that," replied the old landlady. "I 'ope I can tell a gentleman from a mere common person. Some people look down on sailors and such-like, but I'm not one of that sort. As I often say, where would Old England be without 'em!"

"'Hurry up with that supper," said Mr. Bell.

"Shall I lay for two, Mr. Merriweather?" asked the old lady.

"Course not! I'm only one."

"But the lady?"

"What lady?"

"Why," she said, "your wife!" Mr. Bell pulled the handle from the door and stood looking at her blankly. The landlady gave a gesture of self- reproval. "That's me all over. I forget what I have said and I forget what I have n't said. What I ought to have told you before blurting it out like that was that I 've discovered your wife, Mrs. Merriweather, in Grundy Street; that she's simply overjoyed to 'ear of you, and I 've asked her to come 'ere this evening."

"Then," said Mr. Bell solemnly, and shaking the white door-handle in the old lady's face, "you jest listen to me. You 've asked her to come 'ere; you can jest jolly well ask her to go away again. I'm not goin' to see her."

"Well, well, well," said the amazed landlady, "'ere's a pretty how-d'ye-do! And she talked so affectionate about you, too, and she says, 'Oh!' she says, 'I do so long to look on my sweet one's face again.' I had the least drop of spirits with her, and we drank your very good 'ealth."

"Very kind of you," said Mr. Bell doggedly, "but that don't affect my position. When she comes, you get rid of her, and, in future, don't you go potterin' about and mixing yourself up in my affairs, because I won't have it. See? I 've got plenty to worry about," added Mr. Bell fiercely—"more than you think for— and I don't want no interferin' old cat—"

"When you 've quite done using language," interrupted the old lady, bridling, "p'raps you'll kindly put back that door-'andle where you found it. Letting you my ground-floor front for a paltry four and six a- week don't entitle you to walk about with bits of it in your 'ands. So there, now!" She went towards the kitchen, soliloquising. "Interferin' old cat, indeed. I'll learn him!"

It was an hour later that Mr. Bell, by dint of staring hard at a model of H.M.S. Temeraire weathering a gale on a furious sea of blue linen, came to the decision chat there were no means known to civilisation by which he could compel the proprietress of the Climax Tea-Rooms to recognise his rights. He pitied himself sincerely, and, indeed, that seemed the only action that he could take without incurring some risk. She was, he knew, an obstinate young woman.

"You might as well argue," muttered Mr. Bell disconsolately, "with a brick wall."

He would have to find a berth and live on as a bachelor, contenting himself with an occasional cup of tea at the rooms and the opportunity of listening to her. He would have to comport himself, too, with respect, or she might forbid him to enter the doors even as a customer. Mr. Bell had returned to the table and was thoughtfully finishing the remainder of his supper when a knock came at the door. His landlady shuffled through the passage to answer. He rose quickly, and opening the door, took off the handle, closed the door again, and listened anxiously.

"Is my long-lost 'husband in?" asked a high strident voice. "I 've left me glasses at home, but no doubt I shall recognise him."

"Come inside, Ma'am," said the landlady in injured tones, "and let me shut the door. Your 'usband, I'm sorry to say, has got a 'nasty temper."

"I 'll temper him," said the loud-voiced lady, "if he comes any of his cheek with me. He's been away from me for six year, and the least he can do now he has come home is to apologise."

"Spoke like a true woman. Ma'am," remarked the landlady applaudingly. She tapped at the door. "Mr. Merriweather! Mr. Merriweather! Open the door. 'Ere's your wife come to see you."

"Go away," shouted Mr. Bell, "and don't be a silly juggins."

"That voice!" exclaimed the new arrival ecstatically. "Oh, I could swear to it amongst a thousin'!"

"Come, Mr. Merriweather," called the landlady in appealing tones, "open the door like a man."

"I ain't her husband at all," bawled Mr. Bell. "Tell her to be off home again, and leave me be."

"Oh," cried the lady pathetically, "he disowns me! Oh, that it should have come to this! Oh, that I should have lived lo see this day! Oh, that—oh, that—"

"She's faintin'!" screamed the landlady. "If you are a man, and not a block of wood, opin the door, Mr. Merriweather, and lend me a 'and!"

Thus appealed to, Mr. Bell opened the door. His landlady was endeavoring to support a very large woman whose eyes were half closed; she carried a small shiny bag, from which a cork peeped shyly. Mr. Bell assisted to drag her into his room, and his landlady, with an adroitness that did her credit, found a flat bottle in the visitor's shiny bag, and extracting the cork first, sampled the contents herself and then pressed them upon their owner. That lady, after taking a long sip, sat up limply on the chair and looked around vacantly.

"Where am I?" she asked feebly. "Has there been a accident?"

"No, dear," replied the landlady; "there ain't been no accident; it's only your nerves that have give way."

"You'll be as right as rain," said Mr. Bell, "when you 've rested a bit."

"That voice again," said the lady dreamily. "Can I be awake?"

"She identities you," remarked the landlady with a triumphant air.

"Shut up your nonsense," begged Mr. Bell uneasily. The recovering woman's eyes wandered round the room slowly. "You 're jumpin' at conclusions, you are, and it's only makin' her worse."

"Walter!" tried the lady, starting up. "Oh, Walter! Has the sea give up its dead?"

"No," said Mr. Bell, struggling to escape from the large woman's embrace; "it ain't."

"You 're altered, loved one," said the large woman pathetically, "sadly altered; but I knowed you at once. Oh, how thankful we ought to be for this precious moment."

"'Ere!" protested Mr. Bell, "take your arms away from my neck!"

"Never, Merriweather!" she cried. "Never so long as life's left in me!"

"Make her leggo," cried Mr. Bell. "She's strangling of me."

"And who," she said, releasing him, "who, Merriweather, has a better right?"

"Lot of use putting on clean collars." grumbled Mr. Bell, adjusting his necktie. "Now have a good look at me, and tell the truth, and put a end to all this misunderstanding."

"That was always his amusing way." explained Mrs. Merriweather to the landlady. "I don't suppose there was ever his equal for a joke—not this side of Aldgate, at any rate."

"Joke or no joke," said the landlady, "I'm amply repaid for all my trouble by seeing you two brought together again. And as I daresay you 've a lot to talk about, I 'll leave you alone for a bit."

"If you go from this room," declared Mr. Bell aggressively, "I shall jump out of the window."

"He's overcome with joy, I expect," whispered the landlady. "He don't know whether he's on his 'ead or his 'eels. I 've seen 'em took that way before now. He 'll calm down presently, I shouldn't wonder."

"There 'll be precious little calm about," cried Mr. Bell furiously, "if you two women don't get out of my room. 'Ere am I worried 'alf out of me senses about another—another affair, and you come 'ere jawin' and cacklin' and faintin'—"

"Merriweather!" said the large lady impressively, "look me in the face."

"Whaffor!"

"Look me in the face and answer me true. I can bear it. We women are used to suffering—"

"I'm sure!" murmured the landlady, sniffing.

"And I only want to know the worst. Tell me the truth, and I 'll leave you in peace."

"I'll tell you anything if you 'll only do that."

"have you," asked Mrs. Merryweather formally, "have you got yourself mixed up with Another?"

"Yes," said Mr. Bell, "I have."

"Lead me to the front door, Mrs. What-is-it," requested the large lady in a pained voice. "My 'eart is full of woe and bitterness against the world. To think that I have found him only to lose him again! My grief is more than I can bear. Never, never, never in this world shall I be seen to smile again! Is there anything left in the bottle?"

The landlady found the flat bottle, and Mrs. Merryweather sipped it, making a wry face, as though it contained the most repugnant and displeasing of restoratives.

"Lean on my shoulder, Mem," said the sympathetic landlady. "Shows you what men are."

"But don't you fancy," cried Mrs. Merryweather at the doorway, with a sudden outburst of fury, "don't you imagine for one single moment, my fine fellow, that you 're going to get off scotfree. Don't you let me leave you with the idea that you 're going to have it all your own way. I 'll keep my eyes on you—such as they are—and I 'll never let you have one moment's peace."

"'Earear!" said the landlady.

"You shall never be free from me. I 'll track you, if needs be, to the uttermost ends of the earth. I 'll put the County Council on you. I 'll watch you and foller you, and denounce you night and day. I 'll give up the rest of my life to showing you up in your true colours. I 'll—I 'll—"

"Go on," said the landlady in an encouraging way, "let him have it hot."

"No," said the large Mrs. Merryweather tearfully, "I can't say no more. I'm but a poor, weak woman, and I love him in spite of all."

"Bye-bye," said Mr. Bell, with a fine affectation of indifference. "Mind the mat."

Mr. Bell, after a sleepless night, rose early and succeeded in finding work at an engineer's in Canning Town. The long sea-voyage had aided the change in his features by tanning his complexion, and when at the shop he met a man with whom he had once worked in Rotherhithe, and this man, so far from recognising, gave him a history of old acquaintances whom he called "softs"—a gallery of foolish gentlemen in which Mr. Bell was at once hurt and gratified to find that he himself figured—then he no longer feared detection. After work he went home and washed and apparelled himself with care, and slipped away quietly without another encounter with his landlady, who, however, put her head out of the first-floor window and called after him.

"'Ound!" screamed the landlady.

At the Climax Tea-Rooms he took his seat near to the door, jerking his head carelessly in acknowledgment of his wife's business-like smile. He ordered tea and a poached egg from the head assistant, noting the while furtively that his wife behind the counter was watching them both.

"Nice row I got into over you," whispered Caroline, as she brought the metal teapot. "Don't look at her, or else she 'll think we 're talking about her, you see."

"What's the trouble now?"

"Oh!" said the young woman confidentially, "it was all about last evenin'. After you was gone, you see, I 'appened to say in course of conversation, you see, what a nice face you had, and— Don't you go getting conceited, mind!"

"I'll take care," promised Mr. Bell, interested. "Go on!"

"And so I was talking about you, you see, and quite by chance, I remarked that if you come in again, you see, I should set my cap at you."

"Very 'armless remark."

"Upon which," whispered Caroline tragically, "upon which she flies into a passion, you see—calls me everything but a lady. I answers back, you see, and end of it all was I give her a week's notice, you see."

"I'm sorry there's been this upset," said Mr. Bell with a gratified air, "all on my account."

"Oh, it's nothing!" said Caroline lightly. "Plenty of places open for a good worker like me."

"Do you mind doing me a great favour and earning at the same time a pair of kid gloves?"

"Seven and a half," remarked Caroline, beaming.

"Mind talking to me in rather a friendly way while I'm 'ere this evening?"

"Give her the needle, won't it?" said the girl sportively.

"That's what I mean," said Mr. Bell. "It 'll learn her a lesson."

"Keroline," called her mistress sharply, "come 'ere this minute."

Caroline obeyed, but soon found an opportunity to make her way again in the direction of the doorway, where she gave Mr. Bell two violets to place in the button-hole of his coat, and made several remarks in a tone of voice that managed to reach the burning, indignant ears of young Mrs. Bell. Such as: "Oh, you are a tease!" and "If you say I'm nice-lookin' again I shall slap your face!" and "I expect you 've said all that to a lot of gels before," and other phrases of similar import. When Mrs. Bell could endure this no longer she came from behind the counter and ordered Caroline to take her place, saying that she herself would look after the tables.

"Good evening. Ma'am," said Mr. Bell.

"Oh!" said Mrs. Bell, "good evening."

"Been a nice, bright day."

"Thought it seemed rather miserable."

There was a pause. Mr. Bell, under cover of an evening paper, reached out and touched her hand. She did not reprove him, and he pressed her hand; whereupon she seemed to realise the situation, and moved it away quickly.

"Busy, Louiser?"

"Are you comfortable where you 're lodging?" she asked sharply.

Mr. Bell drank deeply from his thick cup before answering.

"I don't think," he said, "I do not think, that I knew what comfort was before I went there. I'm waited on hand and foot; the landlady couldn't be more attentive if I was one of the family. I think I 'm very fortunate in 'aving hit on such a 'appy home."

"Is she young?"

"Depends on what you call young," said Mr. Bell evasively. "Anyhow, I promised her I wouldn't be late back this evening; so, with your permission. Ma'am, I 'll pay up and take my departure. Will you call the good-looking gel that waited on me?"

"No!" said young Mrs. Bell. "You needn't pay for what you 've had."

"Pardon me," he replied with laborious politeness, "I prefer to pay as I go. There's sixpence; and that 'll be a penny for Caroline."

"If you don't take it up at once," she said heatedly, "I 'll throw it out into the road."

"That's your look-out, Ma'am. Where did I put my hat?"

"You needn't be in such a hurry," urged Mrs. Bell, fingering her pinafore-bands nervously. "I 've been thinking that I could afford to pay back that money soon, and so, if you returned to England in a few years' time—"

"My landlady's waiting."

"Let her wait," cried the young woman. "What right's she got to expect you to be at her beck and call? Why don't you be independent?"

"How can I?" asked Mr. Bell, "when I'm dead?"

She moved her slippered foot agitatedly on the floor and bit her lips. Mr. Bell found his hat and rose. She glanced at him, but he preserved his stolid expression and commenced to hum a sea-song. From outside the swing-doors there came the sibilant whisper of women's voices, changing to louder tones as the two doors pressed open. Large Mrs. Merryweather entered first and looked around in a short-sighted manner, as she fumbled with her spectacle-case.

"My husband 'ere?" she asked loudly.

"Your husband," replied Mrs. Bell, "is not here."

"A lie!" exclaimed Mr. Bell's landlady, following in; "nothing more nor less than a low lie. There he stands, a-shrinking and a-cowering like the 'ound he is!"

"I ain't a-shrinking," declared Mr. Bell valiantly, "and I ain't a-cowerin'."

"Merryweather!" said the large lady, "one last appeal I make to you. Before I call upon the lor to help me, give in to the promptings of the heart and return to your home. If it's a hot supper you want, you shall have it. If it's your pipe you want, you can smoke it now all over the 'ouse. If ever I was 'arsh with you in the old days, we 'll let bygones be bygones, and begin afresh."

"You 'll excuse me," said Mrs. Bell, trembling, "but will you kindly let me know what you 're jolly well talking about?"

"Come 'ere," said the landlady to Mrs. Bell privately. "I 'll explain it all in two words."

"Don't you interfere."

"It's a case," persisted the landlady, "of man and wife meeting after what you may term years of absence, him being seeposed to be dead, and her thinkin' she was a widow. And it's me that's brought 'em together."

"Do you mean," said Mrs. Bell, pushing the old landlady aside, "to look me in the face and tell me that this is your 'usband?"

"Isn't his name Merryweather?" inquired the large lady.

"Never you mind what his name is. You put on your glasses"—here Mrs. Bell with a trembling hand turned up the gas until it whistled madly—"and look at him well, and then tell me the truth—if you can," she added.

"I had them in me bag last night," said Mrs. Merryweather as she fixed her spectacles, "only they'd got underneath the bottle." Mr. Bell put on the serious air of a man about to be photographed. "Now let's see."

"This 'll prove it," said the landlady with confidence. "This is the last act, this is."

"Mrs. What-is-it!" exclaimed Mrs. Merryweather feebly.

"Yes, deer!"

"There 's some 'orrid error. This ain't my husband at all."

"Nonsense!" said the landlady. "Take another look."

"I don't want to take no more looks," said the large lady tearfully. "My dream of joy is o'er. Take me away, take me away! How far is it to the Eastern Hotel?"

"Now," said Mrs. Bell to the landlady, "now, perhaps, you 're satisfied, Ma'am!"

"Far from it," declared the exasperated old woman as she piloted her charge to the door. "Far from it, Ma'am. He may chuckle and he may sneer and he may crow, but he's somebody's 'usband, and I don't spare trouble, breath, nor time until I find out whose."

"I must be getting along," said Mr. Bell.

"Wait a bit, Robert," commanded young Mrs. Bell. "Before you two ladies go on to the public-'ouse to have your—"

"Medicine," moaned Mrs. Merryweather.

"Allow me to inform you that this gentleman is my 'usband; and that anybody that goes interferin' with him has got me to reckon with."

"Jest my luck," said the old landlady gloomily as she went out. "I'm always losing lodgers."

"And I s'pose I'd better move along home, Louiser," remarked Mr. Bell when the two ladies had gone.

"Don't be so foolish," said Mrs. Bell, patting his cheek. "You're at home now."

A MODEL CRIME

The two swollen-eyed men from Bethnal Green rubbed their stubbly chins thoughtfully with the palms of their hands. They glanced at the yellow young man in the armchair, and then out of the window at Jermyn Street. The yellow young man was Mr. P. Rawlings, from San Domingo, and these were his chambers.

"Wot d'ye mike of it, Jimes?"

"It's thick," whispered James, hoarsely. "Vurry thick, Awlbert."

"T'ent as though this gent wanted the other gent abslootly mide off with," urged Albert.

"I should strongly object," interposed young Mr. Rawlings from the armchair, in his thin high voice, "if anything of the kind were done. Understand that, once for all. There must be no great harm done to Mr. Burleigh. He is simply to be kept out of the way for a month. He proposes to start shortly for a quiet trip on the Continent, and—"

"Before his merridge," remarked James.

Mr. P. Rawlings threw his black cigar into the fire with an impetuous exclamation.

"Be-fore his merridge," echoed Albert.

"He must be abducted and kept quietly for a space until I give the word," said young Mr. Rawlings.

The two men glanced at each other again.

"He's a biggish chep," remarked Albert.

"Chlorryfom might do it," said James, thoughtfully. "But it's a precious risky job. Do you 'appen to know the lidy he's going to merry, sir?"

It was a most unfortunate question.

"What the devil has that to do with you, man! There is your business. Mind it."

Mr. P. Rawlings was in a great rage. He had started up from his chair, and stood glaring with his small black eyes at the two men.

"No 'arm done, sir," said James, in a conciliatory way, "I on'y asted the question. I wish to Gaud he wasn't a M.P., that's all. They're such a fussy lot, and you see he's a important chep. Why, I see his portraits are in the shop-windows, and he's in Madame Tussaud's, and—"

"I know, I know. It makes me hate him all the more."

"Got to be done to-night, has it, sir?"

"This very night. He walks round St. James's Park between nine and ten. What you ought to do is—"

A long detailed explanation. The two Bethnal Green gentlemen listened with great attention, nodding now and again as sign of their acceptance of the suggestions.

"If I were abroad," said Mr. P. Rawlings at the conclusion, "this could be done as easily as the striking of a match."

"Ah!" said James, bitterly, "that's just where it is. You're in 'appy England now, the home of the free, where for the leastest little thing a man finds hisself locked up. Still, we'll do wot we can, won't we, Awlbert?"

He closed his left eye for a moment as he looked at his colleague.

"We will that," responded Albert. "The best of men can do no more."

"You understand," said Mr. P. Rawlings, decidedly, "that I give you nothing now. Come back here this evening and take me to the place where he is, and the money is yours."

"I could have done with a bit on account," said James.

"Not a penny," said Mr. Rawlings, definitely.

The two Bethnal Green gentlemen sighed a protest against the dogmatism of Capital.

"Well, if you won't, mawster," said Albert, philosophically, "I suppose you wont."

The House that evening was unusually full. There was some excitement in the air, and earlier in the afternoon the Inspector had shaken up nearly a helmet full of tickets for the Strangers' Gallery. The space dividing Ministers was littered with the strips of paper which members tear up when they are in an emotional mood, and no one was perfectly asleep. The youthful-looking member who was addressing the House came to his peroration. He glanced at a small red bonnet in the Ladies' Gallery.

"For my part, Mr. Speaker, I can only say, that so long as life remains with me—and that period may be short, and it may be long—I shall not cease to present with all the vigour in my power the arguments to which the House has so generously listened this evening."

Enthusiastic cheering, as Mr. Gerald Burleigh resumed his seat. Congratulators nodded from the front bench of his own side. A pleasant little note of felicitation tossed across from the opposite side. Young Mr. Burleigh, M.P., hurried round to meet the small red bonnet.

"You are going for your usual walk round St. James's Park, I know," said the Red Bonnet, pleasantly.

"No, I am not, dear. I'm going to stroll with you on the terrace."

"Well," the Red Bonnet gave a sigh as affectation of regret, "it is useless to argue with a Member of Parliament. I only hope that my cousin—Bother!"

Mr. P. Rawlings, blinking his small black eyes, said he was pretty middling. How was Mr. Burleigh? Burleigh, without answering, said that Mr. Rawlings's cousin and he were just about to stroll on the Terrace, so that they would have to say good-bye to Mr. Rawlings.

"Burleigh," Mr. Rawlings took the young member aside. "I want to speak to her as a member of the family about money matters. I want to do something rather handsome for her when this affair of yours comes off."

"You're very good," said Mr. Burleigh. He said this unwillingly, for he usually told the truth. "But, really, I don't know—"

"No, you don't. I'm not so bad as you think, Burleigh. I've got a heart after all, although my manner is a little odd at times. Now, you go for your usual run and I'll talk to her."

Mr. P. Rawlings insisted on walking out of St. Stephen's and across the yard with Gerald Burleigh. He seemed to talk rather quickly, and with a dread of anything like a pause in the conversation. Outside the gates he stopped.

"I must hurry back to my cousin," he said. He looked across the road and took his scarlet silk handkerchief from his pocket. The two Bethnal Green gentlemen standing on the opposite side of the road saw this, and then, shading their eyes, looked up at the clock. "You won't be more than half-an-hour?"

"Less," said Gerald Burleigh.

And striding across the road, St. James's Park way, he disappeared from sight.

"Nah, for this desprit deed," said James, with much good-humour. "Is Ginger in Birdkige Walk with his keb?"

Albert nodded, and smiled the confident smile of a general who sees success.

"It's the biggest old beano I was ever in," he said. "I will sy this for you, Jimes. You're a perfect mausterpiece."

Mr. P. Rawlings did not return to his cousin. Instead he took a swift cab to his rooms in Jermyn Street, and, arriving there, walked up and down outside. He was in a great state of nervousness, and he managed, in peering anxiously towards the end of the street, to drop bis pince nez and smash the glasses.

"Well, I'm hanged!" said Mr. P. Rawlings. Which remark was, of course, premature.

A cab drove up. On the top was a long orange case, corded up. Out of the door stepped James; James, in a state of much disorder, red stains on his band, a look of extreme fright on his swollen countenance. Albert behind him trembling obviously with horror.

"Well," said Mr. Rawlings, with an attempt at cheeriness, "you're soon back. You've managed it, I hope?"

"Yus," said James, hoarsely. His voice sounded like the voice of a blanket. "Yus, we've managed it. For Gaud's sike, sir, go upstairs."

Mr. P. Rawlings did so. He left the door open for the two men to follow, and switched on the light in his rooms. He picked out a particularly strong cigar, as though to honour the occasion, and stood the liqueur stand on the table. Then, with his back to the fire, he awaited their coming.

"Mind the corners, Jimes," said Albert "Lift your end, cawn't ye?"

"Aint I aliften my end?" said James, in a hoarse whisper. "It's bloomin' 'eavy. Nah then, al-together! That's it."

They brought in the long case and placed it carefully on two chairs. Mr. P. Rawlings started forward.

"Stand back, sir," whispered James. "Don't touch the 'orrid thing until you've 'eard the tile. Awlbert, shet the doar."

"What on earth have you got there?" cried Mr. Rawlings, excitedly.

"He's not on earth," said James, reverently, "He's in 'Eaven, poor chap, or 'Ell as the kise may be. Can't you turn the lights dahn a bit, sir?"

There was a break in the voice of the Bethnal Green gentleman. He untied the cord as the yellow Mr. Rawlings and the trembling Albert stood by. Albert poured out some port in a tumbler; James turned over the top lid of the case and lifted a handkerchief from the end.

"Great God," cried Mr. Rawlings. "You've killed him!"

The two men took their caps off reverently as they looked with every sign of remorse at the placid face, Mr. Rawlings gazed at the smoothly parted hair, the neat moustache, the strong chin, the—

"Tell me what it means," he cried, feeling for the broken pince nez. "Why have you done this? Why have you brought him here?" The two men did not answer. "Do you know who you are? You are"—he gave the word in a muffled scream—"murderers."

The two men started as Mr. Rawlings, half white now and half yellow, hissed the word at them.

"It was an oversight, I admit," explained James, slowly. "I s'pose we used too much chlorryfom. But if you're going to call us nimes, mister, perhaps we can find a title or two for you."

"What is it to do with me?"

"A prutty tidy bit," said James, with much decision. "For one thing we're a goin' to leave Mr. Burleigh here, and we're a goin', Awlbert and me, to give ourselves up at Vine Street. There's nothing like being perfectly strite forward in these matters. And your nime will be mentioned as 'aving egged us on to the deed."

Mr. Rawlings screamed. He rushed to the door and turned the key.

"You have done this purposely," he exclaimed. "You blackguards."

"We didn't do it purposely," remarked Albert, setting down the tumbler; "but we cert'ny are blaiguards. All free of us are."

"Come on, Awlbert," said James, "It's no use arguing the question. Let's get down to Vine Street and see the Inspector. How might you spell your nime, mister?"

"Look here," young Mr. Rawlings breathed quickly. "Look here. I'm going away. I am going to leave London at once."

"No daht," said James, ironically. "O no daht. And leave us two gentlemen to bear the brunt of it all."

"You have only to—to dispose of the body," said Mr. Rawlings, appealingly. "You can easily do that."

"Ho, yus,"said Albert. "Nothing easier I'm sure." He laughed a short sharp laugh of derision. "It's quite a everyday job this is."

"Look here," cried Mi. Rawlings. He laid a hand on James's sleeve in an imploring manner. "If I give you"—he whispered a large sum—"will you get rid of it? I shall catch the morning mail at Charing Cross, and go right away—for good."

James hesitated. He drew Ins colleague aside, and conferred with him.

"Look 'ere sir. We're lettin' you have it all your own way, I know, but if you'll double that figure, we'll—well, we'll do wot we can."

"And you will take this—this away?"

He looked with loathing at the ghastly upturned face in the long wooden box.

"No cheques mind you," said James, with sudden suspicion.

"Notes and gold, my good man, notes and gold."

The transaction took but a few minutes. Then the two men lifted the long box and carried it slowly downstairs.

"Give us a 'and, Ginger," said James to the red-haired cabman. "The gent don't want it awfter all."

A yellow frightened face watched them between the curtains of the first floor window. The cab drove off slowly and solemnly St. James's Street way. At the corner it stopped.

"There's on'y one thing now," remarked James. "How are you going to get rid of the body of this onfortunate young Member of Parliament."

He laughed with the satisfied air of a man who has done a good night's work.

Albert considered.

"Tell ye wot," said Albert, "I'll tell ye wot. Tike it back to the Marylebone Road where we pinched it from; stick it outside the blooming Exhibition and let old Tussaud, or wotever hisnime is, find his property there in the morning. Is that good enough?"

James slapped his colleague on the knee.

"My boy," answered James, with much good-humour, "it's great, I never have give back anything before as I borrowed, but just for once, I'll do it."

MERRY SPRINGTIME

He was not (said Mrs. Bosnell) what you would call an attractive-looking gentleman, but, so far as I am aware, there is no law to prevent anyone from having a sturdy figure and rather prominent ears, if they care to do so. He had an agitated way with him on the occasion when he called to ask if I'd got a room to let, and I suppose it was partly this which made me say "Yes!" without thinking. On the moment, he stepped inside, hung up his soft hat, and murmured to himself "Sanctuary, sanctuary!" I have heard people say grace in a less thankful manner.

"Your name, sir, please," I asked, glancing at the blank label on his suit-case.

"Darling," he ejaculated.

I told him pretty sharply he was not to talk to a woman of my age in that way. He answered that he shared the surname with a well-known judge. I mentioned the inclusive terms per week, and he agreed to them so promptly that I half wished— But I shall know what to ask another time.

My two daughters came home from business that evening at the usual hour, and their young gentlemen called in at their usual hour. Your girls of to-day can always find fault in anything their mothers do, and mine declared I ought not to have taken Mr. Darling without references. They appealed to the gentlemen, who, very wisely, declined to take sides, and some argument followed, and went on until a knock came at the door.

"Mrs. Bosnell!" called Mr. Darling.

"Yes, sir?" I said.

"Would you mind asking your visitors to make less noise. I can't get on with my writing."

"I'll give them a hint, sir."

My daughters quietened down. They admitted Mr. Darling had a pleasant way of speaking, and this was in his favour; the great point was the discovery that he wrote. Both Muriel and Queenie are gone on books, and it has always been a desire with them to meet an author. They wondered whether he chanced to be a bachelor. The young gentlemen believed that, in a general way, authors were married men, but, on being challenged, were unable to give any reason for this view; one said that most of them gave way, sooner or later, to drink, and Queenie remarked that genius was entitled to certain peculiarities. We laid the table for supper, and Queenie went up to tell Mr. Darling the meal was ready. She returned with her eyes nearly bolting out of her head.

"He's evidently," she announced in a whisper, "in what is called the throes of composition." I suggested the cough mixture that I always pin my faith to; Queenie and Muriel exclaimed, "Oh, mother, you are, really!" and I held my tongue. Mr. Darling, it appeared, did not want supper, but wished for an evening newspaper. Queenie's young gentleman took a penny from the mantelpiece and went along to the newsagent shop; when he came back he mentioned that cricket was opening well. Queenie snatched the journal from him and glanced at the headlines. We all looked over her shoulder.

"There you are!" she cried, pointing to one of the columns. "What did I tell you?" It was headed "Strange Disappearance of a Novelist." I took the newspaper upstairs when we had had a read and a good look at the portrait; it was a snapshot, rather blurred, and conveyed nothing in particular. Over supper we discussed the matter. Muriel's young gentleman said, "Wait. Do nothing until a reward is offered," and this was carried, as they say at committee meetings, verb. sap.

I felt somewhat worried about it all, but interested, too. Mr. Darling (to keep to the name he had first offered) gave little or no trouble, and a more considerate lodger I could not wish for. He kept to the house all day, and strolled out only in the evenings, and on these occasions muffled himself up around his neck, and pulled his soft hat well over the eyes. Whilst he was out, the girls and myself went through the contents of his suit-case, more out of curiosity than anything else, and Queenie pointed out that he owned no less than two fountain pens. The foolscap sheets on which he had been writing were torn up; Muriel said it was a shame to think a masterpiece had thus been lost to the world. The suit-case contained a photograph, and my girls said that the lady seemed to have a will of her own.

Something else of importance happened in London, and the newspapers, after the early burst of information, made no further comment on the disappeared novelist. But the matter became talked about in our road; it is just likely I threw out a hint to the party next door when we were setting the washing on the clothes lines. Folk began to call who had never called before, and eventually Mr. Challin barged in. Mr. Challin, having retired from the Post Office Savings Bank, had nothing to do but to interfere in matters which did not concern him, and he told me, in his brusque way, that he was going to have the mystery cleared up.

"For all we know," he said resolutely, "the chap may have a wife and children, all broken down in health, owing to his departure from home. They may be at death's door. They may be on the edge of going out of their mind."

"He's unmarried. The newspaper said so."

"That makes it worse," declared Mr. Challin, "because it deprives him of any excuse for vanishing. Anyway, I'm going to have a talk to him."

"Not on my premises," I said.

"Is he in at the present moment?"

"At the present moment he is not in."

"Then he must be out," said Mr. Challin. "Consequently, I shall take up position near to yonder gate, and stay there until he returns. I must bring all my persuasive powers to bear on the man, and, if necessary, I shall use force."

"Mr. Challin," I said, "you are nothing more nor less than an old meddler."

"Mrs. Bosnell," said he, "take care you don't bring yourself within the law of libel."

I watched from the ground floor window, and sure enough when Mr. Darling returned, carrying his evening journal under his arm, the fusser engaged him in conversation. Mr. Darling appeared to be nervous, but he stood his ground and shook his head definitely. Mr. Challin called to a policeman who was going by. The three argued. Mr. Darling suddenly opened his newspaper and indicated a paragraph. The constable said something to Mr. Challin, who lifted his hat apologetically to Mr. Darling.

"Tell me," said Mr. Darling, coming in, "who is that extraordinary person who has been talking to me? Do you know, Mrs. Bosnell, who he thought me to be? He had the impression that I was the well-known novelist who has apparently been missing for some days. Very complimentary, no doubt, but I had to show him the news that the party in question had returned home, after a brief and quiet holiday in the Isle of Wight."

"People about here, sir," I remarked, "are fond of getting strange ideas into their heads. My advice to you is to take no notice."

My two girls were terribly disappointed. It seemed they had given private hints to other young ladies in the warehouse, and obtained a good deal of esteem and respect in consequence; they had to face the necessity of offering some explanation. Queenie felt certain, in spite of the discovery of the writer person, that Mr. Darling was, in some way or other, connected with a mystery. Queenie's young gentleman agreed with her view, and said we all ought to form ourselves into a committee for the purpose of keeping an eye on our first-floor back, and thus giving assistance to the law. I said that if I found myself attending a police court, I should, in all probability, expire of the shock before starting out. Meanwhile Mr. Darling paid his bill for the week and told me he was well satisfied.

Mr. Challin, when I caught sight of him from the window, looked very sorry for himself, and I hoped the blunder would be a lesson to him. He was everything a retired Government official could be; what I mean to say is, he had been elected on the borough council, and he was a guardian and a school manager, but he still had the leisure to attend to other people's business, and to write notes to the local paper about every blessed subject he could think of, and to attend public meetings and call out "Question!" It was on the Wednesday afternoon of Mr. Darling's second week with us that Mr. Challin, in going by, beckoned to show that he wanted to talk. I had some idea of turning one of the rooms out, but the charwoman had not arrived, and I was glad of an excuse for postponing a start. I went to the gate.

"I have solved the riddle, Mrs. Bosnell," he said pompously.

"Which one? The one about why does a sheep—"

"I have discovered the explanation," he went on, "of your so-called Mr. Darling's real identity. The particulars came to my knowledge quite by chance, and the description given to me absolutely tallies."

The charwoman was coming along from the tram-lines, and I told him to cut a long story short. Put in a few words, Mr. Challin's news was that a boxing man who had arranged to fight another boxing man at a place in Holborn was missing. Nothing had yet appeared in the newspapers, but folk who were in the know had acquaintance with the facts, and private inquiries were being made.

"Well," I interrupted, to put the charwoman off the scent, "all I can say is, Mr. Challin, that if the rates go up much higher, some of us will know how to vote when the next election comes round. Good morning!"

I was certainly under the impression that my woman had not caught anything of the matter we had talked about, but she very soon put me right on this. Her husband, it seemed, took an interest in boxing, and, in fact, did nothing else for a living. The running away, she said, of the pugilist in question was a serious affair for his backers, and they were hunting high and low to discover him, and to induce him to face his opponent. Mr. Darling, at this moment, was out on what my daughters call the lawn, at the back of the house, and he appeared to be going through some kind of gymnastic exercises.

"That proves it!" said the charwoman. I ordered her not to jump at conclusions, and to refrain from saying a word on the subject outside my house.

The two girls, that evening, were naturally astonished, but when we had debated the matter thoroughly, they agreed Mr. Darling did look more like a fighting man than anything else. They spoke about his ears; they now understood why his hair was cut so short. There came a ring at the door, and Muriel went to answer it, because it was just the time for her young gentleman to make a call. A scream from her called me and Queenie, and we rushed out to find a mob—nothing less, I give you my word—a mob trying to force a way in. I flung one of the shortest down the steps, and a man, edging forward, announced they had come on a peaceful mission. He instructed the others to keep quiet and remain outside, and we gave him permission to enter the house.

"A friend of mine, ladies," he said respectfully, "has took up his abode in this 'ere domicile. All I ask is to be allowed to favour him with one minute's conversation. That over, I guarantee you won't, be further disturbed, or worried, or incommoded."

He marched up the staircase. He came down in less than the minute.

"Lads," he said to the crowd, "we've made a bloomer. He's no more like Bat Jenkins than I am like the Prince of Wales. Bunk off!"

You would have thought that Mr. Challin, as a busybody, had been sufficiently discouraged to leave us and our first-floor back alone. Not him! The girls had gone to bed, and I was locking up, when I heard the flap of the letter-box give a clip. Outside I heard Mr. Challin's cough as he tiptoed away, and something assured me more trouble was afoot. In the letter-box I found a copy of a police notice headed "Murder." It gave a description of a man who was wanted for a crime at Shepherd's Bush, and finished by announcing a reward of a hundred pounds.

Mr. Darling came down to the kitchen in the morning, whilst I was still in my disables, and said, with a cheerful manner, that he would have his egg poached. I had scarcely slept a wink all night, and my nerves were not what you would call first-class.

"Tell me," he said at the doorway, and glancing back at the pictures which had been taken down in the passage, "this horrible and exasperating business of turning out rooms in a house—how long does it generally last? I happen to be new to it."

"A week, sir. Or ten days at the utmost."

"Mrs. Bosnell," he said, "in that case, I am going home to-day. Going home to my wife. Her spring domestic industries are, or should be, over, and if you can give me a written document to prove that I have stayed here all the time of my absence, I think she will understand and forgive. By the by, I see in this morning's newspaper they have caught that Shepherd's Bush man. Our London detectives are pretty smart, aren't they?"

MR. AND MRS. RANGER

"Wipe your boots well," commanded Mrs. Ranger insistently from the "kitchen, "bring your overcoat through to the scullery, 'ang up your hat, and walk quiet."

A large, mild-looking man, with his face set in a frame of light whiskers, came obediently on tip-toe through the passage. Mrs. Ranger, looking up from her desperate work of ironing, frowned at her husband.

"Ah!" she said bitterly, as she took a fresh iron from the fire and placed it perilously near to her plump cheek to test its warmth, "I see what you want to do. You want to wake up baby."

"I can't altogether say," replied Mr. Ranger, with the cautious air of one anxious not to irritate by direct contradiction, "as I do."

"Oh, yes, you do," she declared emphatically; "and don't you go hinting that I'm a story-teller the moment you put foot inside the 'ouse." Mr. Ranger, in the scullery, sighed. "What's it you say?"

"Never said nothing," he replied soothingly.

"That's your low artfulness," retorted Mrs. Ranger. "If you were anything like a man, you'd answer a civil question when it was put to you."

She ironed hard for a few minutes, not feeling sure of her argumentative ground; but when Mr. Ranger, having washed his face at the sink, reappeared, she was again ready for the attack.

"What makes you home so early to-night?" she demanded.

"Committee meeting didn't last long," explained her husband. "I'd got everything ready for 'em, and they'd only got to agree with it all."

"And the rest, I s'pose, are drinking away in public-'ouses like anything, and never giving a thought to their poor, 'ard-working wives at home."

"Well, my dear," he said genially, from the fireplace, "they ain't 'usbands of yours."

"Don't throw that in my face, John," she said pathetically. "I know as well as you do that I could have made a better marriage than I did; but don't, don't—"

"What I mean to say is—"

"I know what you mean, John," she said tearfully, "but I don't think you ought to turn against me. It's bad enough when I go home on Sundays and take baby, to hear my sisters talk. 'Well, Emily,' they say, 'whatever you could see in the man beats me.'"

Mr. Ranger hummed a cheerful tune and opened the evening paper.

"I suppose I must have been off me 'ead," said Mrs. Ranger, as one anxious to find excuses for grievous error. "I can't account for it any other way." She turned a white garment, pressed heavily on the iron, and ran it up and down. "If you'd been good looking, I could have understood it."

Mr. Ranger laughed.

"I was never what you'd call a pretty man," he said jovially.

"If you'd had a pleasant manner about you," went on Mrs. Ranger, "that would have been something. As it is," here she touched her eyes with a corner of her apron, "as it is, I'm simply a laughin'-stock for one and all."

"I say, my dear," protested Mr. Ranger, "really!"

"Oh! a lot you care!" she cried fractiously, and applying herself again to her work. "I tell you, I'm getting pretty well tired of it. There's only one good thing about it," she said, with gloomy hopefulness, "it can't last after I'm dead and gone."

"Shall I read to you?" asked Mr. Ranger submissively, after a pause.

Mr. Ranger selected a column in the back page of his evening paper, a column in which unexpected aphorisms had for next-door neighbours a cookery recipe or a hint on fashions.

"'It is stated,'" read out Mr. Ranger, "'that black velvet will be all the rage during the ensuing season; it will not, however, be worn by—by débutantes.'"

"By what?"

"By—by débutantes," repeated Mr. Ranger doubtfully.

"Don't you dare refer to such creatures!" ordered Mrs. Ranger solemnly, and Mr. Ranger proceeded, in a chastened tone—

"'An old Oriental saying is to the effect that a wife and her husband should meet but once.'"

"There's something in that."

"'If all the hairpins that are lost in London during a year were placed on end, they would reach part of the way to the North Pole.'"

"Well, I never!" exclaimed Mrs. Ranger, now genuinely interested. "Is that a fact, John?"

"It's in the paper."

"Wonder where they pick up such things."

"'A useful sideboard,'" read on Mr. Ranger, greatly encouraged, "'may be made by procuring three old orange boxes, staining them the colour of mahogany—'"

"Your mother never said anything more about that chest of drawers of hers," said Mrs. Ranger, reminded of one of her numerous grievances. "That's your family all over."

"Understanding was," he remarked gently, "that you should have 'em when she was gone."

"She don't show much signs of going."

"I'm very glad," said Mr. Ranger slowly, "to say that she don't."

"Oh!" wailed Mrs. Ranger desolately, giving up work and subsiding into a chair, "oh! that it should have come to this. To have a husband who sets himself amongst your enemies, who snaps your head off directly you open your mouth, who hates the very ground you walk on!"

"My dear! my dear!" he protested.

"Don't speak to me, you—you—I don't know what to call you. You don't know how to treat a good wife, you don't."

"But I only—"

"John," she said, with forced calm, "I can't trust meself to talk to you. Go straight to bed at once, before I lose me temper."

This, it is to be observed, was no special occasion in the Ranger household, but merely the usual evening performance. Mr. Ranger, out at six in the morning to the works in Camden Town, and away all day, was engaged sometimes in the evening with business concerning the benevolent society of which he was secretary, and the pent-up conversation of his wife—who declined to mix with her neighbours in Charles Street—found itself culminating by the time he reached home, and was thereupon poured down on his patient head as hot lava from a volcano. This had lasted now for a year or two, but although experience had dulled the first feeling of resentment, Mr. Ranger was still far from the point where enjoyment is situated, and the almost certain knowledge that he would be met by upbraidings made him a quiet, reticent man during the day, so that one or two of his colleagues began to doubt him, suspecting secret mismanagement of the society's funds, the only thing in their opinion likely to make a man thoughtful and reserved. The habit of nagging should have been checked in Mrs. Ranger at the start; this remedy had been neglected, and she now comported herself, with rare exceptions, as though she were the least happy of wives—this in spite of the small baby whose efforts to amuse on Sunday afternoons would sometimes conquer her, on which occasions the Ranger household found peace under the beneficent rule of the infant autocrat. When the baby relinquished his position, and retired to his bassinette, the normal condition of affairs was resumed. Once or twice to Mr. Ranger came the thought of flight to a distant land, but he pushed this aside; he did, however, leave home suddenly one Saturday evening on the excuse that he had heard disquieting news of his mother's health. He kissed the baby, and would have kissed his wife, but she, disappointed in her evening's exercise of words, dared him to do so, and he sighed and went out.

Half an hour later two men called at the house in Charles Street. On Mrs. Ranger answering the door, they inquired in an important whisper whether Mr. Ranger was at home.

"Then he's got wind of it, Bill," said the first man, on receiving the answer.

"So long as he's got clear away," said Bill mysteriously, "we needn't grumble."

"We're friends of your 'usband's, ma'am," explained the first man.

"Pot-house friends, I suppose," retorted Mrs. Ranger.

"Not exactly," said the first man patiently. It seemed as though this type of wife was no stranger to him. "I wouldn't go so far as that. Can we step inside the passage for a moment?"

The two went in and closed the door.

"Anything you've got to say, say it sharp," requested Mrs. Ranger. "I've got work to do."

"To break it gently to you, ma'am," said Bill, "there's a warrant going to be taken out against Ranger for embezzling the funds of our society."

"Which of you is it that charges my husband with that?" demanded Mrs. Ranger.

"It isn't either of us," said the first man hastily. "It's a chap named Wilks, a man that personally I can't stand the sight of."

"He's too hasty, is Wilks," corroborated the other. "He runs past himself."

"Wilks got an idea into his head—"

"First one he ever had there."

"That your 'usband's accounts were all wrong, so he goes into them with one or two other equally woollen-'eaded members, and they report that everything's at sixes and sevens. They goes, therefore, to-morrow, they does, to the police court, swears black's white and white's no colour at all, and a warrant'll be issued. We hears of it, Bill and me—"

"I 'eard of it first," said Bill.

"And we puts our 'eads together and we says, 'Let's give him the office,' we says. 'Let's give him a chance of getting away.' And here we are."

Mrs. Ranger turned up the little oil lamp with an unsteady hand.

"I'm much obliged to you," she said quietly. "I sha'n't forget your kindness."

The two men, who could take upbraidings with calm, showed confusion.

"Where's he gone to, ma'am?"

"I haven't the slightest idea," she said steadily.

The two resumed their hats, and one opened the door.

"You can count on us, ma'am, if he gets caught."

"But he sha'n't be caught," said Mrs. Ranger. And closed the door after them. She ran upstairs and, as a first step, had a good cry, silently, because baby was asleep. Then she felt capable of seeing everything clearly. Ranger had probably not gone to his mother's—that announcement was part of the ruse—but there was a chance of finding him through that address, and hurrying to the telegraph office, she despatched a wire, ordering him on no account to return home. There remained other precautions to be taken. The man named Wilks had once paid some attentions to Mrs. Ranger's sister, but an economical habit of paying for nothing had prejudiced him in the eyes of the young lady, and his dismissal had incensed him against the family. To her sister Mrs. Ranger hurried by tram, and, the safety of the small boy at home urgently in her mind, hastily arranged a scheme with her young sister by which Mr. Wilks was to be asked to join a party on Monday, at ten o'clock in the morning, to go to Chingford. As to the question of expense, Mrs. Ranger gave her sister half a sovereign, and told her to convey with the invitation the fact that the trip would not cost Mr. Wilks anything; he would be unable to resist this, and Ranger would at least have another day to make himself secure. Returning home with all speed, she found that her boy, awaking in her absence, had roused the district with his appeals for the presence of a mother; that a neighbour had left her own children, who were ill, to soothe him.

"Thank you," said Mrs. Ranger, in the awkward way of one unused to give this form of recognition. "I'll do as much for you some day. How're yours?"

"Not more than middlin'," said the neighbour dolefully; "what I hope is that it's nothing catchin'."

There was money in the Savings Bank, and all of this could be withdrawn in a day or two and placed somehow at her husband's disposal. This might enable him to get abroad somewhere. She and baby could follow later. Thinking out the details on Sunday, it suddenly occurred to her that she had considered no plan which necessitated their separation; that, despite all the bitter remarks she had made to him, she was now only anxious to see him safe and be with him again. Indeed, she reproached herself already for her unkindness. This, probably, had driven him into confusion with his accounts, and a desire—say—to back horses. It was always betting that ruined secretaries. On Monday morning she received a post-card from him.

"Shall not return just yet. Thanks for telegraph message. Love to baby and you."

Mrs. Ranger was found, to her great confusion, in the act of kissing this card, when a knock at the wall from her neighbour signified that her presence was requested in the back garden.

"It's scarlet fever," said the neighbour, weeping, "and they've all got to go away."

"So sorry."

"I thought," sobbed the neighbour, "I thought I'd tell you, because—because, you see, I went in to see your little boy the other night—"

Mrs. Ranger flew away from her and closed and locked the scullery door. She ran upstairs with a confused fear of finding her baby in the last stages of illness, but that young gentleman, engaged in manœuvring a tin train, met her with cheerfulness, begging only that she would for just one moment assist him in his labours by acting as tunnel, a part that could be played by any adult prepared to go down on hands and knees. But slightly reassured by this, she undressed the baby, subjecting him to a close examination, which he, as one full of the responsibility and worry of conducting a railway, felt bound to resent. He was astonished out of powers of speech by finding himself at this hour of the morning placed in bed and evening prayers said over him with unusual fervour. Master Ranger began to have fears for the sanity of the world.

The economical Mr. Wilks had been caught by the bait thrown out by Mrs. Ranger's sister, and the two men who had called on Saturday night called again to inform her secretly that no application had been made at the court that morning. They were extremely anxious that Mrs. Ranger should on no account tell them where her husband was, so that they might, if occasion required it, swear an affidavit of ignorance without a blush. They also comforted her to some extent by informing her that there had been a "whip round" amongst the dissentient and anti-Wilks members, and that with the money thus obtained it was proposed to procure the services of an accountant of repute, gifted with an ability to tell good figures from bad. So far as Mrs. Ranger was herself concerned, it appeared to her not very material whether her husband were guilty or innocent; her duty was to help him. Despite her worries, she could not help recognising that she now felt towards him as she had done in the old days of courtship. He possessed her thoughts as he had not done since that time. One or two wives whose husbands belonged to the society, and to whom the information had been dutifully repeated, called during the day to offer condolence.

"They're all alike," said one wife at the doorway, disappointed at not being asked inside, where discussion could have lasted an hour or two with comfort. "The more you 'ear about them, the more convinced you get that there isn't a pin to choose between 'em."

"I mustn't detain you," remarked Mrs. Ranger politely.

"Me time's me own," said the caller lightly. "As I was saying, this world wouldn't be so bad if it wasn't for the 'usbands."

"I'm sorry you're in trouble," said Mrs. Ranger.

"I wasn't thinking of myself. I was thinking of you."

"Me?"

"Why, yes," said the astonished caller. "Everyone knows how he's treated you. I don't wonder you used to speak your mind pretty plain. Other people used to blame you, but I—"

"My good woman," said Mrs. Ranger impressively. "Listen to me. Me and my husband were always very fond of each other, and if we ever had any words, it was my fault."

"Think what you're saying," implored the other woman.

"It was my fault, and I don't care who knows it. He's always been the best of husbands to me, and when this little affair is explained—"

"That'll take a bit of doing."

"Good morning," said Mrs. Ranger shortly, "and thank you for calling."

"You'll never," promised the caller solemnly to the next lady whom she honoured with a visit, and to whom she repeated this conversation, "you'll never find me doing a kind action again."

The Rangers having been at one on the question of thrift, it appeared that the amount invested in the Savings Bank exceeded the amount which Mr. Wilks had announced as the total of the defalcations. Mr. Wilks, having slightly over-eaten of gratuitous food at the Epping picnic, was indisposed for a day or two, and in his continued absence progress in the matter of police court proceedings was stopped. Mrs. Ranger contrived an elaborate scheme whereby her husband could proceed from his mother's house to Milford Haven and take thence a steamer for America; she wrote to him briefly, giving these directions and ordering him on no account to reply, but to act instantly in accordance with her instructions. Master Ranger showed continuous interest in his railway business and, for a baby expected to sicken with a grievous complaint, exhibited considerable sprightliness, expressing now and again a keen anxiety to see his father, thus causing tears to come very near to his mother's eyes. She waited anxiously and without much hope for the accountant's report, and when news came that Mr. Wilks had recovered from his severe attack of indigestion, she braced herself for the worst. The ship by this time would have left South Wales, and she thought continuously of her husband making his lonely way to a strange land. A single knock that came to her door on Thursday evening made her leave the doctor, who had called to see the baby, and hurry downstairs.

"John!" she whispered affrightedly.

"I ought not to have called," admitted Mr. Ranger humbly.

"You should have been on your way to America," she cried, pulling him in and closing the door.

"You told me to go, I know."

"Then why didn't you go? Why are you here now?"

And the lamp being out in the passage, Mr. Ranger, to his intense astonishment, received a hug and a kiss.

"I say," said the surprised Mr. Ranger, "do you know who I am?"

"You're my dear husband," whispered Mrs. Ranger. "But they sha'n't catch you."

"Well," he said good-humouredly, "we should look a bit silly if they caught us like this. All the same, give us another kiss."

Another knock came, and Mrs. Ranger, pushing her husband into the front room, locked the door and, holding the key behind her, went to answer it.

"It's all right, Mrs. Ranger, ma'am," said the two men.

"That there Wilks," added one of them, "is nothing more nor less than a—" He refrained from a description.

"The accounts are not wrong, then?" cried Mrs. Ranger.

"Come out right to a penny."

"'Ere," said the voice of Mr. Ranger from the front room, "who's saying anything about accounts? Let me out!"

"There's been a little misunderstanding, old man," explained one of the men, as Mr. Ranger reappeared.

"I'll misunderstand you," he threatened, "if you suggest there's anything wrong with my accounts!"

"It was Wilks."

"Well," said Mr. Ranger, "I'll Wilks him! And as I guess from what you say that there's been a lot of trouble over it whilst I've been away attending to my old mother, I'll resign."

"But we're going to subscribe and give you a silver teapot."

Mr. Ranger wavered and looked at his wife. She replied with a glance of appeal.

"Very well, then," he said. "Under the circs, I agree. But, mind you, no more Wilksing."

When the deputation had returned thanks and withdrawn, and the doctor had assured them that Master Ranger had been much too artful to catch the dreaded epidemic, an idea suddenly occurred to Mr. Ranger.

"Let me see," he said thoughtfully, "did I have that second kiss or did I not?"

"I really forget, John," answered Mrs. Ranger demurely. "But as I owe you a good lot, perhaps I'd better—"

"Pay up," suggested Mr. Ranger.

MR. BARLING'S INCOME

It had been an imperfect year for Mr. Barling, but it would be a hard year indeed that frowned continuously, and last night, for the first time, luck had smiled upon him. The smile had come in the singular form of a railway accident. Not a serious accident, but with little to do but to catch flies in his City office, it was better than nothing. Mr. Barling had wired to the company's office, and now, well wrapped up and his face touched with artistic white, sat in his flat in Ashley Gardens and awaited the arrival of the company's representative.

"Can you see a gentleman, Sir?"

"Who is it, James?" asked Mr. Barling.

The excellent James whispered—"I rather fancy he's from the railway. Sir, in answer to that message that I—"

"Show him in, James, but tell him that I am very, very ill."

Mr. Barling closed his eyes. A jovial, breezy man, in a short coat and a silk hat, advanced into the room with an air of repressed exuberance.

"My name," said the jovial man in a forced whisper, "is Drayton. I 've called to make some inquiries—"

"I know—I know," said Mr. Bailing feebly. "This is a terrible thing, this accident."

"Most deplorable, Sir."

"Physically," said Mr. Barling, speaking with a great effort, "I'm—I'm a wreck. Mentally, I'm an extinct volcano."

"Dear, dear, dear!" said the breezy man, clicking his tongue. "Is it so bad as that?"

"It's worse," sighed Mr. Barling.

"And what compensation, Sir, did you think of asking, I wonder?"

"Take a cigar," said Mr. Barling desolately. "I shall never smoke again; you'd better take both of them."

"These smokes," said the visitor cheerfully, as he lighted up, "weren't bought at no five a shilling, I'll bet my boots."

"You were talking about compensation," said Mr. Barling brokenly. "I daresay now"—here he had a fit of imitation coughing—"I daresay the company will want to settle it by a lump sum at once."

"Shouldn't wonder."

"And to enable them—oh, my poor head!—to enable them to arrive at a figure, I suppose—" Mr. Barling stopped, and looked round the room vacantly. "Where am I?" he asked. "Where was I?"

"You were supposing, Sir."

"Ah yes. I suppose it will be necessary to give some idea of my income during the past three or four years."

"That's just what I want to get at," said the visitor, taking out his pocket-book and blinking as the smoke came into his eyes.

"Roughly speaking," said Mr. Barling in a weak voice, "I 've been making three thousand a year—perhaps more."

"Perhaps less?"

"No less," said the invalid, with sudden vehemence, "not a penny less."

"Very well," said the man cheerfully, making an entry in his pocket-book; "not a penny less, then."

"Besides that, there have been various odd affairs that have brought in money. Suppose you say four thousand."

"Four thousand,' repeated the visitor, as he made the correction.

"I 've also had money left me at various times," went on Mr. Barling, with fine exaggeration, "running into, say, about five or six hundred a year. Suppose we say five thousand in all."

"By all manner of means, Sir."

"I dareday," remarked Mr. Barling, "that, if anything, I 've rather understated it. But I'd rather do that than appear to be trying to get the best of anybody."

"Rather."

"If the company likes to offer me a big lump sum down—I shall be wrong, perhaps, in accepting it; but still— Well," continued Mr. Barling, with a burst of generosity, "one ought to be straightforward, even when one is dealing with a railway. What shall we say to five hundred pounds down and say no more about it?"

"I should reckon," agreed the visitor, "that that would be letting them down cheap."

"Five hundred guineas," remarked Mr. Barling thoughtfully, "paid down at once. Not later than the end of this week. Next week I want to be off to—I mean to say next week I may be a good deal worse, and then I might want a bigger sum if the matter remained unsettled."

"If I were you. Sir, I should get all I could out of them. See how they treated me the other day, when I happened to be in a second-class carriage with a third-class ticket! Why, charged me excess!"

"What?" cried Mr. Barling, "you don't mean to say that they made you pay!" He laughed cheerfully, and forgetting his pained whisper, spoke in his usual loud voice. "Well, well," he said, "if they'd do that they'd do anything. Fancy coming down on you."

"I was very much annoyed about it, Sir. It was only a matter of threepence-halfpenny, but it's the principle of the thing that I look at."

"Fancy charging you," repeated Mr. Barling amusedly. "One of their own— Well, it just shows that one needn't be too delicate in charging them. Have the other cigar."

"I 'll put it in my pocket," said the visitor, rising, "and smoke after lunch. Meanwhile, perhaps, you won't mind filling up this form and sending it on to me."

"With great pleasure," replied Mr. Barling. "You'll tell them how bad I am, won't you? And do you mind letting yourself out? I can't move hand or foot, as you see."

"Good morning. Sir!" said the visitor, backing to the door, "and thank you for the information."

"My good fellow! " said Mr. Barling handsomely, "don't mention it."

The man was but half-way down the steps when he stepped aside to allow two people, who had just arrived, to pass by him. At the same time he heard the voice of Mr. Barling from the landing above. Looking back, he saw that gentleman descending upon him furiously.

"You scoundrel!" screamed Mr. Barling. "Wait where you are!"

"Meaning me, Sir?"

"Yes, you." Mr. Barling had flown down the stairs in his scarlet dressing-gown with remarkable activity. "What the deuce do you mean by leaving this form on my table? As sure as my name's Barling—"

The two new arrivals stopped and looked on at the dispute.

"What's all this fuss about, Sir? I call on you in my capacity as Income Tax collector. You very kindly give me ample information—"

"Do you mean to tell me that you didn't say you were from the railway company?"

"Railway company?" echoed the Income Tax man indignantly. "Why, what on earth are you talking about? It was you that—"

The two new arrivals begged pardon. They were from the railway company, they said, and one of them, a doctor, expressed his great satisfaction at finding that Mr. Barling was none the worse for the regrettable accident of the night before.

"Bah!" said Mr. Barling.

THE RESULT OF MISS KNIGHT'S TEMPER

The Hall was filled with a talking, noisy audience; some of the men were smoking a pungent kind of tobacco that induced the ladies on the platform, who had come from west to south-east, to cough and to pat their eyes with lace handkerchiefs. Miss Wareborough, the good-looking young woman in the chair, tapped at the desk with her ivory hammer more than once to appeal for attention to the speech of Mr. James Flanders; and Miss Wareborough, as she did this, looked like a young woman who was in the habit of being obeyed. Added to this was a thoughtful look, because she remembered that the last time she had come to the Hall someone had looked after her; someone who was now away in West Africa. The Hall watched her closely.

"Come in her broom, she did. She 's a toff, mind ye."

"Don't she do her 'air up nicely too! I wish mind 'd behive itself like that. Why—"

The girls who were talking received each a tap on the shoulder.

"Can't you keep quiet when anyone 's makin' a speech," inquired Miss Emma Knight, "or won't you?"

The girls ceased their conversation, but they told each other in a whisper that Emma Knight thought she was everybody because she had saved a few pounds and was engaged to this young man now speaking; but that Emma Knight was not everybody, and, what was more, Emma Knight never would be everybody. The loud, strident voice of the young man on the platform moderated itself slightly as, approaching the end of his speech, he turned, with an awkward attempt at courtliness, to the young woman in the chair.

"One word, friends, in conclusion. Before we finish this meeting of the Social League, there 's one duty we have to perform. We have to offer our 'earty thanks to the—well, charming ladies who 've sung to you this evening; they 'aving taken the trouble to come from their comfortable mansions, and what not, to give you an entertainment that's good enough—though I say it—for the 'ighest of the 'igh. (Cheers.) It don't do to pick out names; but to you, Miss Wareborough, for occupying the chair (Loud cheers), we tender our 'earty thanks, and we 'ope to see you again. By your grace of manner, by your charm of disposition, by your attractive—"

Mr. James Flanders, looking round the crowded seats for a word, encountered suddenly the large eyes of Miss Emma Knight. Miss Knight's breath was coming quickly; there was a look in her eyes that made young Mr. Flanders falter.

"What I meant to say, friends, was that we 're under a debt to all these ladies, and I, therefore, ask you to 'old up both 'ands to signify your acknowledgment. All in fiver of a vote of thanks to—? All! Carried unanimous."

Miss Emma Knight, waiting for Mr. James Flanders in the Hall, nodded rather curtly to her friends, and seemed to have no desire to exchange conversation. This was odd, because Miss Knight was, in an ordinary way, adroit of repartee, and it is notorious that those gifted in this way are seldom reticent. She crossed over and looked through the thick diamond-shaped windows of the Hall. Outside she saw the figure, rather blurred to sight, of Mr. Flanders, in no hat, seeing the ladies into their carriages; saw Miss Wreborough turn to speak to him, and caught enough of the words to tell that it was an invitation to Eaton Square.

"Thought as much," said Miss Emma Knight under her breath. "I 'll Honourable Miss Wareborough her, if she ain't careful. Let her stick to her own spear of life, and not come interferin'." She turned as someone approached. "Oh, you 'ere? Thought you 'd forgot me."

"Course I have n't forgot you," said Mr. Flanders, fanning his heated face with his soft hat. He was flushed with the strain of observing etiquette. "Not likely to."

"I 'm not so sure," snapped Miss Knight. "Seem to be paying everybody else a lot of attention."

"How you do talk," complained the young man. "You see how busy I was."

"Just what I did notice."

"I 've got a lot to look after a evening like this, and if I don't see to it all no one else will. When ladies come down 'ere from the West-End—"

"Pity they don't stop at home," said Miss Knight bitterly. "Be more to their credit. Asked you to her place for one evening, didn't she?"

"She did so."

"Ah," said Miss Knight mysteriously, "I 'eard! I don't miss much. I 'm not quite blind. I wasn't born the day before yesterday. Old enough to begin to take notice, anyway. I may be a fool in many things, but—"

"You 're 'aving a rare old recitation all to yourself," said Mr. Flanders good-humouredly. "Shall I see you home ?"

Miss Knight affected a kind of icy surprise.

"Me?"

"Yes, you, Emma."

"But I don't live in Eating Square!"

For answer Mr. Flanders, the Hall being now nearly deserted, snatched a kiss, an adventure that oftentimes he had found an effective peacemaker. On this occasion it so far failed that Miss Knight rubbed her cheek laboriously and then walked out of the Hall alone.

"'Pon me word," said poor Mr. Flanders, "girls do take some managing."

He made hurriedly some arrangements for closing the Hall and ran after her. Just by East Street he managed to check her hastening footsteps.

"You ain't going like that," said Mr. Flanders appealingly.

"How am I going then, clever?"

"Look here, Emma. You know as well as I do that I don't care for anybody else but you. What 's the sense in being so jealous about nothing at all?"

"I beg your pardon," said Miss Knight coldly. "I 'm not in the least jealous. Quite the reverse!"

"And as regards Miss Wareborough; why, she 's engaged to a young Lieutenant out in West Africa."

"Be more to the purpose if you knew his name."

"But I do! Their coachman told me the last time he was down. Lieutenant Wyndham is his name, and the town he 's at is Benaro." Miss Knight, with less acerbity, requested that the name of the town should be spelled to her, and her command was obeyed. "And rough times they 're going to have by all accounts. Sooner him be out there than me. Why, those blacks—"

"Never mind about the blacks," said Miss Knight, allowing the young man to take her arm. "We needn't trouble about them. All we 've got to do is to look out for ourselves. If everybody minded their own business we should be a lump better off."

"Can't say I agree with those principles, Emm'a," he said submissively; "my tenets are rather different to that. I 'm what's called an altruist."

"I don't call myself names."

"An altruist is seeposed to be a chap—"

"'Scuse me interrupting," said Miss Knight. "The next is my turning. And so you 'll give up all idea of going, James, to see this Miss whatever-her-silly-name-is?"

"She 'asn't fixed a date yet," he said evasively.

"But when she does?"

"Well," urged Mr. Flanders apologetically, "it 'll give me a insight into high class life, you see, Emma. There 'll be a lot of swells there, and her mother, and—"

"I wish you a very good evening," said Miss Knight icily. And turned sharply away.

It was a source of great perturbation to Mr. Flanders (who was really a very good fellow, with a habit, perhaps, of taking himself rather too seriously) to find that for some days Miss Knight studiously avoided him. One showery morning he passed by her in the turbulent crowd that attacks trams and 'buses near the Elephant and Castle; and she nodded, and remarked cheerfully, "More weather!" and went on her way Citywards. Mr. Flanders was astonished at this behaviour, and he stood still and watched her green hat as she gradually disappeared with the crowd in the London Road. He was, indeed, so dazed by the incident that he found himself whirled in a strong stream of people upon a Tooting tram—his desired destination being Cambervell—and went some distance before he realised the error. Usually he was an expert and a careful facia writer; but that morning, over a shop facing Camberwell Green, he outlined the words "Emma Knight" instead of "Robert Henry Batten," the name of the shop's proprietor, and found himself the object of much badinage in consequence.

He walked home in the evening, surveying South London with a gloomy air, and was not even cheered, as was commonly the case, by the sight of his name as hon. sec. on a small printed bill in a confectioner's shop. On the mantelpiece of his room he found a square envelope, addressed in a definite handwriting that he had seen once before.

"I wish I 'd never run across any of these swells," said Mr. Flanders gloomily, as he looked down the letter. "It 's all very well to talk about mingling of classes, but it don't seem to be a dazzling success so far as I 'm personally concerned. And, furthermore—"

Mr. Flanders stopped, and his countenance brightened as he read the postscript—

"I think I heard that you were engaged. If this is so, will you consider this invitation to apply also to the lady? My mother and I will be pleased to make her acquaintance."

In three minutes Mr. Flanders was at the door of Miss Knight's house. In another minute Miss Knight's mother and Miss Knight herself were in possession of the astounding information that that young woman had been formally invited to Eaton Square.

"Seems to me, Emma," said her mother, bewildered, "more like a bit what you read of in novelettes than anything real. It 'll take your cousin Jane Emily down a peg or two, at any rate."

"I don't know as we won't go in a cab," said James reflectively. "It 'll look better than a 'bus."

"Budford Street 'll stare," said Mrs. Knight, with relish. "It 'll give the neighbours something to talk about for monce. If I was you, Emma, I should simply borrow those yellow slippers from that girl in your ware'ouse; my brown cape you 're welcome to, as you know. And as regards your 'at—"

"I see by the papers," said James, "that there's more trouble a-brewin' out where her young gentleman is. I expect it 's a rare anxious time for her. That part of Africa, mind ye—"

"We ain't talking about Africa," said Mrs. Knight impatiently; "we 're talking about 'ats. And considerin' that you take your 'at off the moment you're in the 'ouse, what I suggest is that we should ignore the question of your 'at and throw all our thoughts on to the question of your blouse. Now I see some in Box's in the Camberwell Road only yesterday; a kind of an electric blue that ought to look very classy be gaslight, and they were only priced at one-and— Goo' gracious! Why, what's the matter with the girl?"

"Yes, what 's wrong, Emma? Ain't sorry she invited you, are you?"

"I ain't—ain't sorry she's invited me," sobbed Miss Knight; "I 'm sor—sorry for what I 've been and done."

"Why, what have you—"

"Oh, nothing!" Miss Knight rubbed her eyes and rubbed her nose and went to the mirror over the fireplace to look dolefully at her reflection. "Nothing special. Only— Oh it isn't worth talking about now. I didn't think she was so nice as she turns out to be. Were those blouses you speak of full in the sleeves, mother?"

It there was a prouder woman in Walworth on the evening of the visit to Eaton Square than Mrs. Knight, that prouder woman would have required a good deal of tracing. Every window within sight was occupied by a bunch of heads; a semicircle stood expectantly near the hansom and the horse as though waiting for the performance of tricks. Mrs. Knight's moments were fully occupied in answering her daughter's repeated inquiry as to whether she looked all right at the back; in giving Mr. Flanders in the sitting-room—sitting-room thrown open to use, bless you, just for all the world as though the day were Sunday—hints in regard to the care of her daughter and the necessity for being home not a minute later than eleven. Mrs. Knight personally conducted the young people into the cab, and with a pride that could not be measured, gave the address to the driver. She slapped an impertinent boy who attempted to interfere with her prerogatives by closing the splashboards, and reopened and closed them carefully herself; and then she leaned over to give a last message to her daughter.

"Mind you take notice of everything, Emma."

At Eaton Square a servant was accepting a telegram from a uniformed lad, and this, as she received with correct formality the young people from Walworth, she handed at once to a young maid in the hall, and the young maid flew with the telegram up the stairs, seeming not to touch them as she went.

"Miss Knight, I think," said the servant courteously, "and Mr. Flanders."

"That 's quite right," said Mr. Flanders. "You go first, Emma."

There were a few people in the large room, and some of them were in a group scanning anxiously the evening papers. A tearful, white-haired, elderly lady came forward and received the confused young people.

"You are my daughter's friends from Walworth," said the white-haired old lady. "She will be down directly. We are all going to have a long talk about arranging bright evenings for your people, and one or two members of Parliament will come in, and we want you both to lead us." The old lady patted her eyes with her handkerchief. "I wished Lilian to put off the engagement, but she would not hear of it."

"Nothing wrong, I 'ope, me lady?" said Mr. Flanders.

"You haven't seen the evening papers? My dear Bertie!" She called to a tall lad in evening dress. "Will you bring me the St. Jameses?"

"Certainly, mother. Here it is." The old lady tried to find her pince-nez, but her son read it for her. "'Terrible massacre at Benaro. A British mission annihilated. English officers murdered. No survivors.'" The young fellow turned with a concerned manner to the Walworth couple. "You see, the reason this affects us so much is that Lieutenant Wyndham is stationed there."

"I 'eard that," said Mr. Flanders.

"And I 'm afraid—I 'm very much afraid—there's positively no hope. It 's a most fearful shock for my sister, and, indeed, for all of us."

"How 'd it be," said Mr. Flanders nervously, "if me and my young lady friend was to retire and look in again some other evening?"

"By no means," said the silver-haired old lady energetically. "Bertie dear! show this young lady some pictures of Benaro."

Miss Emma Knight trembled very much as she sat down and, the youth acting as guide, inspected the photographs. There was one in the book of a square-shouldered, good-looking man in Lieutenant's uniform.

"Is that him?" asked Miss Knight.

"That is Wyndham."

"He's a fine-built young man."

"Shocking thing, don't you know, to think that those beastly blacks have done for him. He was an awfully good sort, and my sister was very fond of him. We all were."

"Was he fond of her, Sir?"

"Why, yes. They were to have been married this autumn."

"Been engaged long, if it isn't a rude question?"

"Known each other all their lives."

"When might this affair have 'appened at the place that begins with a B?" asked Miss Knight in a low voice.

"About a week ago, I think."

A broad, important Member of Parliament was announced, and he came in rather as though he were a hurricane. It was then that Miss Emma Knight made an astonishing remark. She delivered the pronouncement with the seriousness of one making a formal declaration on oath.

"I don't believe," said Miss Emma Knight recklessly, "that he 's been and gone and got killed at all."

Miss Knight's remark sounded more distinctly than she had intended, because just then a hush had come over the room. Miss Wareborough, very pale but very decided, had entered at the doorway. She gave to her mother a telegram from the Colonial Office confirming the news that had appeared in the evening papers; then she turned to greet, gravely but courteously to her guests. For young Englishwomen are still brave, and their hearts, in moments of pain, are for themselves alone.

"We 're sorry. Miss," said Mr. James Flanders awkwardly, "to hear about all this painful bother, or whatever you like to call it, that's resulted in the—"

"Thank you, Mr. Flanders."

"In the sudden, painful, and 'orrible death of—"

"Don't let us talk about it please. How do you do?" (to Miss Knight) "I remember your face at Walworth quite well."

"I remember yourn," said Miss Knight doggedly.

"It is good of you to come to see me."

"It passes an evening away," said Miss Knight.

"We want to do something for the children," went on Miss Wareborough quickly. "I hope you will be able to give us some suggestions. I—I must do something difficult to distract my mind. Anything that will shut out from my thoughts the picture of—"

"I know how you must feel," said Miss Knight sympathetically; "but if I was you, Miss, I shouldn't 'arp on it. I never believe what I read in the papers."

"I wish there was room for hope. The report says very clearly that not a single member of the mission has been saved."

"'Ope on, 'ope ever!" urged Miss Knight.

"Indeed, I wish that I could feel sanguine." She sighed, for the tears were close to her eyes.

"The Government," remarked her brother, "will send out a punitive expedition at once."

"But that will not bring him back," she said wistfully.

"If I might go so far as to express an opinion," said Miss Knight nervously, "which I 'm perfectly aware is a bit forward on my part—"

"Fact matter is," said the Member of Parliament, bustling into the conversation importantly, "these niggers want managing properly. Now my idea is—"

It is all very well for the Member of Parliament to make important suggestions. The Member of Parliament may think he knows the last word about most subjects, but, as a matter of fact, the things in regard to one subject that he does not know would fill a house. For instance, he does not know that up the stairs is flying again the young maid with a letter arrived by hand; he does not know that this letter is from the Great Western Hotel at Paddington. Such is the ignorance of the M.P. on this particular subject that he is unaware that this is from Lieutenant Wyndham, reporting his arrival in England on leave of absence; leave obtained—the note explains—instantly on receipt of an unsigned telegram three weeks since at Benaro informing him in brief terms that Miss Wareborough was in serious danger, and that his presence was required in London at once. The note adds, that as soon as he has changed into the habits of civilisation he will be with them. What the M.P. does presently understand from the confused, delighted drawing-room is that everybody is very happy, and that the conference is to be postponed until the arrival of Lieutenant Wyndham. This information being conveyed by the flying maid downstairs, the cook there is so exuberantly pleased that, albeit a stout lady, she dances round the kitchen and says hysterically, as she sinks into a chair—

"Three cheers for everybody."

Mr. James Flanders and Miss Emma Knight walked home that night because it was a fine night, and, as the young woman acutely pointed out, by walking they would be in each other's company the longer, and, moreover, two 'bus fares would be saved. It had been a most gratifying evening, and the young people from Walworth were content. At Budford Street Miss Knight kissed Mr. Flanders when she said good-night, careless of the fact that neighbours, were watching and that her mother, impatient for report in regard to the evening, was peeping through the Venetian blinds, one of the laths being disarranged for that purpose.

"By-the-bye!" said Mr. Flanders. "Wonder what it cost the party, whoever it was, to send that extr'ordinary telegram."

"Thirty-three-and-six," replied Miss Knight promptly.

"Lot of money!" said Mr. Flanders.

"I don't seepose," declared Miss Emma Knight emphatically, "the party begrudges a single penny of it."

A STORMY PASSAGE

The Mary Beatrice lay at low tide in the harbour waiting for a Paris train, which was picking its way very carefully along the rails on the Quai Chanzy above. The electric globes sent a moonlight haze over the upper deck; the captain on the bridge by their aid looked at his watch and said something about French railways that need not be printed here. A middle-aged clean-shaven, cheerful-looking man sitting on a deck-chair near the funnel glanced up. French children trying to sell mechanical dolls from the edge of the quay, watched casually the melancholy person who walked up and down in a clumsy suit of innumerable fancy baskets, articles which did not appear to be indispensable to the happiness of the evening-boat passengers. At the back, lights of the town speckled the edge of the harbour, and the bell of a tram-car rang warningly.

"Paris train late, surely," said the clean-shaven personage.

"Everybody's late in this country, Sir," replied the first mate respectfully. "Give me England."

"I rather want England myself," said the passenger. "Haven't seen it for ten years." The Paris train stopped on the quay above. Passengers came down the wet stone stairs and advanced to the slanting gangway. "Anyone special on board?"

"Funny thing you should ask the question, Sir. As it 'appens, I see by the luggage that Mr. Lewis home rsham, whose name you 've seen in the papers, is crossing to-night?"

"Don't think much of him," said the passenger, rising and going to the foot of the gangway.

"Well, but, Sir—"

"I am Mr. Lewis Homersham."

"Dang my old eyes," said the chief mate with Kentish strenuousness, "if I ain't always a-putting my foot in it."

The passengers came down the sloping gangway with more or less of trepidation. A tall lady of generous figure, in a flowing grey cloak that made her look like some large bird on the wing, called to her maid in slipping near to the deck end, and the maid, in sympathy, slipped also. Mr. Homersham put out one arm, and with some difficulty saved the opulent lady from disaster.

"Thank you ever so much," she said gratefully. "This is such a very awkward arrangement, and—Martin, how tiresome you are! A clumsier maid I think I never saw." The maid, having picked herself up, ran down recklessly into the arms of two sailors, who caught her and swung her round neatly. "How 's that, umpire?" demanded the two sailors of each other.

"Margaret," said Mr. Homersham suddenly, pulling off his travelling-cap.

"Lewis!" ejaculated the lady.

"But for your voice," he said, "I should not have known you."

"Is that intended for a compliment?" she asked.

"My dear girl," he said hastily, "you cannot, of course, help being charming whatever alterations time may bring."

"They tell me," she said vaguely, as one speaking of a subject of which it was not possible to have personal knowledge, "that I have grown stouter."

"I don't think so," he said. This was not the truth, but it seemed more effective than the truth, for she beamed upon him pleasantly. A family of spare girls, ranging in height from six feet to about four feet two, marched past, clearing the deck and complaining bitterly of the other passengers; the last giant trunk of baggage was being swung on board.

"I have a private cabeen," she remarked, after she had sent a contemptuous look at the thin family, "but I think as I have met you, Lewis, I'd rather stay on deck. It only takes about an hour and a half."

"The time," said Mr. Homersham, "will seem too short in your company."

"Tell my stupid maid to go down, will you, and not to stand there like a ridiculous idiot?"

Mr. Homersham obeyed, slightly modifying the wording of the order, and Martin, giving the patient sigh of one accustomed to dealing with a mistress who possessed a temper, went down the companion. The Mary Beatrice moved gingerly out into the centre of the harbour, where there was just enough water, and seemingly not a tumblerful too much, to enable her to get out into the open. Silhouetted figures lining the edge of the quay waved farewell, the captain ordered a protecting canvas to be fitted at the end of his bridge. Now this startled observant passengers.

"It is going to be a rough crossing, Margaret," said Mr. Homersham, returning. "Are you quite sure—"

"I'm a good sailor," she replied definitely. "I hope you are."

"I hope so too."

"We have an enormous amount to talk about," she said, nodding her large hat in a winning manner. "It seems years since we met, Lewis."

"It is years," he said.

"I was quite a girl."

"You were," he said, "then."

"I saw," she said, "that you obtained your C.B."

"Backstair influence," he said lightly. It seemed that Mr. Lewis Homersham was not entirely at his ease: he assumed too obviously an air of unconcern. "You have no idea how these things can be managed."

"I think I have," she said, touching him on the arm. "I read all about your excellent work as Consul during the outbreak."

"Newspapers have to exaggerate."

"Not unless they see real necessity for doing so. I thought of you a good deal at that time." She paused. The Mary Beatrice had found her way out of the shallow harbour now, and was on the dark open Channel, a fine spray of salt-water came humorously over the first-class deck, and passengers who objected to practical jokes of this kind prepared to descend to the saloon. "I say, Lewis," she repeated, raising her voice, "that I thought of you a good deal at that time."

"You are very kind, Margaret."

"I wonder whether—hadn't you better put up your coat-collar—I wonder whether you have ever thought of me?"

"When I had time to do so."

"Love," quoted the stout lady pathetically, "is of a man's life a what do you call it, 'tis woman's—you must really get some tarpaulins, Lewis. Do bestir yourself, please, and pay some attention to me." A passing sailor with a Red Indian touch in his veins was hunting for palefaces, and brought a covering; the two sat nearer to each other, sharing it. "What was I saying when you interrupted?"

"I 've had rather a busy time out there," he said, without replying to her question. "I ought, I suppose, to have written to you, but the Colonial Office has received most of my letters."

"I wonder whether men ever think," said the lady bitterly, "how much of happiness they miss by concentrating their attentions on mere self-advancement. The day surely comes when they feel remorse."

"One can always find something to reproach oneself about. Are you still living with your aunt in Lancaster Gate?"

"I suppose it never occurred to you, Lewis, that you treated me very badly?"

"I?" he stammered. "I—I treated you badly?"

"You!" she said with calm.

"We had a quarrel, certainly, but—"

"I needn't remind you," she snapped, "who was to blame there. No one can say that I ever began a dispute." He bowed his head politely. "The next thing I heard was that you had left England to take up this appointment."

"May I venture to remind you, Margaret, that you particularly requested that I should do so?"

"My dear Lewis!" protested the lady. "Do you mean to tell me that you don't understand women-folk better than that?"

"I am exceedingly sorry," he began.

"What is the use of being sorry now?" she asked indignantly. "Will that make the case any better? You might go down on your knees before me—"

"The deck is very wet," he urged.

"And apologise for your hastiness, but it would do no earthly good now. The past is past."

"Yes," he said with relief; "it has that advantage."

The Mary Beatrice dipped its head into the turbulent sea. The detachment of spare girls still marching round and around the deck fell into momentary disorder, regaining discipline as the steamer resumed its normal attitude, only to be swept down into the saloon by the next wave. The two were now alone.

"Whom did you marry, Lewis?" she asked sharply.

"I beg pardon."

"I asked you as distinctly as I could, Whom-Did—You—Marry?"

"I have never married," he said, with a touch of pathos in his voice. "I have never been engaged to anyone, Margaret, but you."

"Poor Lewis!" she said. Her gloved hand traced the outline of a heart in the tarpaulin that covered her lap. "And now you are home again, and I am the first person you meet. Some," she remarked with a sigh, "would call this fate." He edged away slightly and seemed half inclined to suggest another name. "There is no doubt, to my mind," she went on in the manner of one propounding a novel idea, "that everything is ordered for us in this world. We are mere puppets; we have to obey the strings that pull us. It is quite useless, Lewis, for you to contradict me because I know that it is so."

"My dear Margaret," he protested, "I don't contradict you."

"Oh yes, you do," said the lady firmly; "you wouldn't be a man if you didn't. And please, please don't pull the tarpaulin away. You can sit closer, surely!" He apologised and edged nearer to her. "I should think, Lewis," she continued, "that when you come to the end of your life the one thing with which you will have to reproach yourself most will be the unmanly way in which you broke off our engagement."

"To tell you the truth, I had nearly forgotten all about it."

"Ah!" she said triumphantly, "I knew it! I knew it! That is how a woman's heart is treated. Lifelong devotion on her part counts as nothing."

"My dear," he said, "do be reasonable. We were only engaged about a fortnight."

"Cast aside like an old glove that has been plucked in the garden of life, and once its petals have commenced to fade—"

"Margaret," he said determinedly, "I can't allow you to talk in this way."

"A man," she remarked acutely, "a man never likes to hear the truth. I've noticed that over and over again."

"Are you sure," he said, after a politic silence, "that you would not prefer to go below?"

"If I did prefer it," she replied brusquely, "I should do so."

"The changing lights at Cape Grisnez," he said, turning his head, "show out very clearly on a dark night like this." She did not look round. "When one thinks of the number of vessels—"

"I suppose," she interrupted, "it is nothing to you, Lewis, that the best years of my life have been spoilt by your inexcusable burst of ill-temper."

"I should be sorry," he said courteously, "to think that had been the case."

"Do I understand you," said the lady icily, "to doubt my word?"

"No, no. Don't misconstrue me."

"I think," she said with deliberation, "that but for your wrong-headedness—but for your fatal hastiness and lack of serenity, we might have spent a lifetime of perfect happiness together."

"Oh?" he said.

"We were young; we could have walked hand in hand through life, sharing each other's sorrows; we should have had every taste in common— You 're not going to smoke a cigar?"

"Do you prefer a pipe?"

"You seriously mean—"

"I was about to ask your permission. The wind will blow it away from you."

"I never tolerate smoke," said the lady, tapping the wet deck with one shoe. "A most objectionable habit, and I do all that I can to put a stop to it. It is never allowed for one single moment in my house. I simply won't tolerate it."

"There is nobody in your house, I take it, who would care to smoke much. For my part, I owe a good deal to tobacco."

"No husband of mine," she said, "shall ever smoke."

He glanced at her curiously. Could it be that she expected a renewal of the old and brief engagement? Were his prospects of a comfortable middle-aged bachelor life in the Albany endangered? Was there not some merciful Statute of Limitations which protected middle-aged men in cases like this? A wave reared its head on the starboard side and broke: the water rolled up to their feet.

"Exactly resembles my life," said the lady, shaking her head dolefully. "Dashed at the very apex of expectation, and all ambition gone!"

"My dear Margaret," said Mr. Lewis Homersham with anxiety, "I really beg you not to talk in this manner. I am distressed to think that you consider your life wasted, but I cannot feel that I am to blame."

"Naturally!"

"I feel sure you have had a fair amount of happiness in your life; that it has not been all so grey as you now imagine."

"I have tried to bear up," she said mournfully. "Nobody knows what it has cost."

"You are still well off, Margaret?"

"Happiness," she said with tears, "cannot be bought."

"Margaret," he said impulsively, "is there anything I can do? You appear to think I behaved badly; can I—"

"Too late," she said with pathos; "too late."

Mr. Lewis Homersham muttered a "Pray excuse me," and started up; before the lady could protest he had marched away aft. This was a situation that demanded insistently the smoking of a cigar; he was a man who thought best when smoking. Her last remark had touched him acutely. Perhaps without knowing it, he had not comported himself in the old days with sufficient tolerance: he might have been hasty, and a right-minded man should repair at leisure the hurried blunders that he makes.

The blustering wind consumed as much of the cigar as he himself did, but he smoked sufficiently to arrange and to make up his mind. It was a wrench to have to alter all his plans; hard on a middle-aged bachelor to have to relinquish his state of single content; but right was right. At any rate, he would renew his proposal on the way from Folkestone to London: he wished he could think there was any chance of receiving a refusal. He wished, too, she had not grown so very stout.

The lights of the Leas at Folkestone were near, and white-faced passengers came up hesitatingly from below. Lewis Homersham, about to rejoin the lady who had once excited his youthful admiration, saw that her maid was now in attendance upon her, receiving stern reproof with a placid aspect of resignation. The Mary Beatrice entered the harbour, and as he took his portmanteau and joined the queue of disembarking passengers, he managed to speak to her.

"You will allow me to travel up with you, Margaret?"

"If you wish it, Lewis."

At the long bench where the Custom officers examined the hand-baggage there was presently commotion. The maid left her open bag and ran to her mistress, who was standing near to Mr. Homersham.

"My lady! They want to charge on those bottles of eau-de-Cologne."

"How dare they attempt to swindle me!" said her mistress excitedly. "Tell them that I shall get my husband to write to the County Council about it."

"You are married?" he exclaimed.

"Yes, yes, of course I am married," she answered impatiently. "Sir Robert had to stay in Paris; it was most annoying; if I hadn't had you to argue with I might have been ill. Which is the way to the train?"

"On reflection," said Mr. Lewis Homersham cheerfully as they went upstairs, "I think I will travel up in a smoking compartment."

THE TEST

"And now," said Miss Hazlewood, glancing at her reflection in a shop window, as the omnibus went down King's Road, "suppose we leave off talking nonsense, and take a serious view of matters. Would you care to be introduced to my people?"

"In answer to your esteemed favour," said young Mr. Manners, "I beg to state that few of the remarks exchanged between us can be correctly described as nonsense. Sentiment, yes. Romance, yes. Love, yes. But nonsense, certainly no. Regarding the second paragraph of your communication, I am willing to take any view proposed by you. As to the third, I have never before heard any allusions to your relatives."

"There is a reason for that." She checked a sigh and gazed ahead thoughtfully. "But we have known each other now for over six weeks—"

"Seems more like six minutes."

"And I think it would be as well for you to brace yourself up to meet them."

"You talk," remarked the young man, "as though it were going to be in the nature of a trying ordeal."

"Some people find them a little difficult," said Miss Hazlewood. "We'll get down at the Town Hall."

"It occurs to me it might be a shrewd and commendable act to give our patronage, instead, to the first house over the way. And if on this occasion you will allow me, my affluent and wage-earning sweetheart, to pay for the two tickets—"

"We have discussed that already," she interrupted. "I earn very good money in Oxford Street—more than you do Westminster way. There is no reason why I should be an expense to you. Apart from that, we are not going to the Chelsea Palace this evening. We are going to a different sort of entertainment. We shall see whether you find it equally amusing."

"My warmest thanks," he said, "for the pains you are taking on my behalf. I have sometimes read of this sort of experience, but I have not hitherto had to undergo it."

She looked at him affectionately and, for a moment only, hesitated.

"You've got to go through with the job, my lad," she declared, "sooner or later, and I have decided that it is to be sooner. Come along!"

They walked along the south side of King's Road, crossed Oakley Street, and presently found themselves in Poulton Street. On the way Miss Hazlewood explained, with something less than her usual business-like self-possession, that her folk were plain folk, and, being plain folk, made no attempt to put on the veneer of courtesy towards strangers. The mind was sound, but, in the general opinion, the deportment scarcely reached perfection. Miss Hazlewood admitted she had, on occasions, taken friends to the house, and they had come away announcing to her a definite intention not to repeat the visit even if offered all the gold held by the Bank of England.

"Didn't you say they lived in Poulton Street?" he asked suddenly.

"Danvers Street," she said, "and I have not hitherto mentioned the address. What made you think of Poulton Street?"

Her companion was about to make an urgent plea for exemption, when a hand gave salutation from a window in Danvers Street, and the owner disappeared quickly in order to open the front door. From that moment Mr. Manners offered no protests.

"Well, Gertie," said the thin woman, in mournful tones, "got another young chap at last, then. Hasn't been for the want of trying that you ain't caught one before. Bring him in and let's have a look."

"This is Fred, mother," said the girl. "Fred, this is mother."

The lady of the house rubbed palm on apron as a preliminary to a hearty and determined shake of the hands. She assured the young man that he was as welcome as the flowers in May, but cautioned him not to expect too much hospitality, for if he did, then he was bound to know disappointment. Times, she said, leading the way to the front room, were not what times had been. The years when the family kept a good table and took beer with supper every night of their lives, were now gone, and she saw no prospect that they would ever return. Her husband, she hinted, felt the deprivation less acutely, because he was able to get his drink at licensed premises where, owing to the fact that he had once been prominent in boxing circles, he rarely found himself called on to pay for his own refreshment.

"You'll find my husband very entertaining," she went on, "—set down, both of you, if you can find chairs you can trust—when he comes in, but if I was you, young man, I wouldn't contradict him. Gertie's father can't bear being contradicted. If he's unable to find words to answer you, he doubles his fist, and then everybody has to look out for 'emselves. He don't stop to think, mind you. He jest lets fly."

"I make no doubt," said Mr. Manners pleasantly, "that he and I will get along well enough together. One has to make allowances."

"I'd rather," she urged, "that you didn't give him anything, mister. If you want to make a loan of any kind, hand it over to me. Don't give to him, whatever you do, or else—"

"Mother, mother!" pleaded the girl anxiously.

"Gertie," ordered the elder woman, with solemnity, "be respectful to your parents. Don't you know what the Bible says about honouring your father and mother? Very well, then. Take care I don't have to speak to you twice; otherwise, you'll know it! Go into the kitchen and see if you can't do some washing up."

In the girl's absence the hostess spoke loudly and more freely. She informed the caller that the circumstance of her daughter sharing rooms with a young lady friend, instead of living under the control and superintendence of a good mother, was one of the most regrettable incidents in a life not free from mental anguish. She declared a serpent's tooth was nothing to it. Not, mind you, that Gertie, in herself, could be reckoned as altogether to blame. Oh, no. Any girl who progressed in the world felt naturally eager to mix with her betters, and in this desire the existence of home was forgotten. As a matter of accuracy, Gertie had not called, before the present moment, for three months—close upon three months ago that she paid a visit.

"Alone?" asked Mr. Manners politely.

The door of the sitting-room was open, and it appeared the door of the kitchen had not been closed. Consequently the young man received nothing more than a wink in reply to his question; the wink conveyed a suggestion that it would be well not to show extravagant inquisitiveness. The lady of the house proceeded to qualify some of the information communicated, and declared that Gertie was a dutiful child, as children went in these days, and perhaps, when she married, the old friendly relations might be taken up afresh. Certainly there would always be a knife and fork for her at Danvers Street, and a knife and fork for her husband; whether in addition there would be anything to eat was a detail in regard to which no guarantee could be made. It depended on office work.

"Are you," asked Mr. Manners, with elaborate surprise, "engaged in an office?"

"I am," she answered.

"Responsible position?"

"If I'm not there to sweep up after the clerks have gone, who else would be likely to do it? As a matter o' fact, I haven't been long back from my work this evening," she went on. "Just at present I'm engaged in a building in Victoria Street."

"Oddly enough, I, too, am engaged in a building in Victoria Street."

"Bless my soul!" she exclaimed, in tones of exaggerated amazement. A thundering single knock came at the front door. "Gertie," she cried, "I'll let your poor father in. Go"—to Mr. Manners—"into the kitchen and have a little 'eart to 'eart talk with her, whilst I have a word with my old lad."

It seemed to Mr. Manners that the girl was not engaged with anything like violent industry on domestic occupations; she welcomed his arrival with a wan smile. The kitchen had two Windsor chairs, and from one he evicted a grey cat. From the other he removed a jug and a thick tumbler.

"And," asked Miss Hazlewood, with an effort at cheerfulness, "what do you think of mother?"

"She strikes me," he answered carefully, "as somewhat—how shall I say it?— somewhat unusual. Perhaps the most unusual person I ever encountered."

"Wait until you see father."

"Is he—"

"He is," she said definitely.

"I suppose," he remarked, "it would not be necessary, when we are married, to see a great deal of them?"

"They would scarcely be daily visitors, but, of course, filial respect has to be thought of. You don't, I hope, ask me to ignore them altogether?"

"We can discuss that later."

"No!" declared Miss Hazlewood, with resolution. "We must discuss it now. I might have kept the two in concealment, but I preferred you should know them, and ascertain for yourself whether or not it affected your proposal to me. It's not too late to back out."

"Gertrude mine," he said, "you are now talking as they talk at Colney Hatch. All the same, I am bound to admit that your maternal parent is not exactly my ideal of a mother-in-law. I can imagine we should not be too well pleased if, when we were entertaining friends, she suddenly barged in."

"Take time to consider it," begged the girl. "I don't want you to do anything you will be sorry for afterwards."

"What I can't quite understand is why, earning the excellent salary you do, you fail to make them adequate grants that would permit—"

The lady of the house apologised for interrupting, and announced that her husband was now ready to give an interview to the young gentleman. "I've told him all about you," she said elatedly, "and you'll find him, sir, as nice as nice can be."

The large man offered to Mr. Manners an enormous hand, saying, "Put it there!" and inflicted a grip which made the visitor wish that less cordiality had been shown. They sat opposite each other, and the large man rested an elbow on an irresponsible round table that leaned over at his pressure. Mr. Manners tendered a cigarette case.

"I've smoked shag all my life," declared the other firmly, "and shag I shall continue to smoke so long as I have the 'ealth and the strength to dror at a pipe. After you with that match, gov'nor." He lighted up. "Now, then"—leaning more heavily on the table—"we don't want no quarrelling, we don't want no disputatingness, we don't want no upset of any description whatsoever. All we want is to know whether you're a-going to act fair and square towards our Gladys."

"Gertrude," corrected the young man.

"If I like to call her Gladys for short"—he spoke with grim deliberation—"do you fancy you're the chap to stop me? Bo you think, for a single moment, I'm going to allow a mere whipper-snapper like you—"

"Keep a civil tongue," ordered young Manners sharply.

"What else am I doing?"

"Being as grossly offensive," he explained, "as you can be."

"You ain't seen me at my best, gov'nor," said the large man, rather taken aback, "or you wouldn't say that. When I make up my mind to be what you call grossly offensive, I'm in the 'abit of using language that turns the air blue for miles. I rec'lect once, when a 'chap was brought 'ere as you are being brought now—" He stopped abruptly.

"Try to comprehend this," directed Manners. "Arouse your sluggish brain and—"

"Now, who's being grossly offensive?"

"And realise that I am not going to allow you to talk to me as you have talked to others. You will speak respectfully, and you will speak decently."

"But see how you're 'andicapping me!" pleaded the man. "All very well for parties of education like yourself to do without what is termed language, but I've got no other way of expressing myself."

"Then remain silent," ordered Manners.

"Sooner than do that, I'd offer to fight you, 'ere and now."

"I'm ready," said the young man.

He took off his jacket. The large man watched intently as links were undone and a sleeve rolled back.

"There's something about you, gov'nor," he said deferentially, "that I admire. You've got pluck, you have. On the other 'and, I've got the science. That's where I should have you, once we cleared the room for a set-to."

"You are over-fat," said Manners, "and over-flabby. It must be years since you put the gloves on."

"I had to give it up," he said, "owing to a weak heart."

"Your heart may be weak, but I'll bet it's sounder than your intelligence."

"Is that," asked the man, puzzled, "intended for a compliment? If so, I accept it, and I assure you, gov'nor, that my one desire is that we may become the best of friends. And now put your jacket on and set down and let me 'ear all about you and this girl of ours. If I went over the mark in anything I said, you must put it down to a father's anxiety. She's our one ewe lamb, and if anything, amiss occurred to her—" He found a grubby handkerchief, and in rubbeeng eyes expressed regret that he had no drink to tender either to his guest or to himself.

He amended this defect later by borrowing a shilling. As he went, he conveyed to Manners his good wishes, and spoke with relish of the treatment he intended to serve out to any beverages provided at the wedding breakfast.

"I like them," announced young Manners to his companion, as they waited for the omnibus later opposite the Town Hall. "A trifle crude, perhaps, but I like them."

"So glad, dear."

"In these times," continued Manners, "when affectation is discovered almost everywhere, it is refreshing to encounter folk who say what they mean and mean what they say."

"And you don't care for me the less because—"

"My love," he cried, "I can honestly say this—what has happened this evening has not in any way diminished my affection for you!"

At the offices in Victoria Street the following night, the charwoman looked in at the draughtsmen's room where Manners was working at a desk. She coughed to obtain his attention.

"Oh, yes!"—detaching himself from the task. "Of course. Settling day. Now, in the course of our previous discussion here, when I noticed that you gave Miss Hazlewood's name as a reference, you mentioned the sum she paid you for pretending, on occasions, to be her mother."

"Seven-and-six, sir. But with everything going up in price—"

"You gave me the wrong address. I had the fright of my life when I discovered we had gone through Poulton Street."

"We moved in a 'urry, sir," she explained, "owing to circumstances. But I managed to let the young lady know. You see, as I told you, she wanted to be loved, sir, not for the money she's earning, but for herself alone, and heretofore the visit has always put the gentleman off. And seeing that, by chance, I 'appened to be able to give you previous information, and seeing that we shan't get the job again—"

He handed over a Treasury note. "Don't bother about a receipt!" he said.

YOUNG PLATITUDE

My friend Platitude—a tall youth of serious appearance and a voice that seems, by some ventriloquial effort, to come from the roof, is gradually obtaining a reputation for shrewd common-sense. People are telling each other that young Platitude has a lot in him, that young Platitude is deep, that the things young Platitude does not know would scarce fill a match-box. I regret to have to state formally that young Platitude is a humbug.

He is an Oxford-made youth, and I think he must have remained in the oven there a little too long, for all the Oxford characteristics have been burnt into him, and will, I fear, never be chipped off. He went straight to a Teaching Centre in the East End when he first came down, and I shall never forget the wise air with which he presided at a series of lectures on Palaentology for the Working Classes. (The place was not really in the East End being, in fact, but a hop, skip, and jump from the Bank; the working classes came to it by underground train from Sloane Square,) He had little to do but to blink warningly at the people who came in late, and to make a few announcements at the end. but these things he did with such a fine air of superiority that people held their breath when they met his eye.

"Have to 'nounce.'" he said once in his head voice after a lecture. "that the—er—usual Tharsday meeting will take place—"

Here he turned over some notes on the table and dropped his pince-nez and re-adjusted them. Everybody craned forward with eagerness to listen to his important pronouncement.

"On Tharsday next," he said impressively.

He tired of the Teaching Centre after a while, and took rooms in an old Inn off Holborn. He told me that he regarded the lower classes as to a certain extent low and added that he thought journalism required a new note. He also said that newspaper writers had got into a groove, and being there—well, there they were, don't you know.

"What the public wants," said young Platitude, in a burst of great confidence, "is something new. Mark my words."

He was kind enough to show me his first efforts in journalism. They included a brief article called "Town and Country": in this it was pointed out that there were differences between town and country, in that towns invariably had a larger population and more houses; a short story entitled "A Mistaken Marriage," that I seemed to have read before, and a four-thousand-word sketch called "Wit in the Olden Days." This latter he thought of sending to Punch; the other two he wanted the Times to have.

"Guvnor takes them in," he said as excuse for this weakness, "and if he likes them he 'll be—er—gratified. What?"

I gave young Platitude no advice, because I knew it was better that he should go through the mill of experience. Later I learned that he had called at Printing House Square with his manuscript, had insisted upon seeing a sub-editor, and the sub-editor had given a frank opinion. Platitude told us that the sub-editor was not a gentleman.

His opportunity came when a friend of his father's, then editing a weekly review, sent him a parcel of six books to notice. I shall never forget young Platitude's air as he sat down to undertake this work. He took three days to complete it, and called into my rooms on the third evening with the result.

"Rather think," he said, with a faint suggestion of relaxing his wooden countenance, "rather think I 've done some deuced good slates."

It is always interesting to read acrid criticism (of other people's books) and I took up the slips of paper with the joy of anticipation. Poor young Platitude!

"Mind you," he urged, as I went through them, "if a man thinks a book's bad, a man ought to say so. When a man thinks a book's good, why then a man ought to say so too."

But Platitude had not said so. What he had said in regard to *this* book was that greater pains would have improved it; in regard to *this*, that the good parts of the book were commendable, while the inferior parts were not commendable; of *this* he had said that no doubt it would meet a long-felt want, always supposing that that long-felt want did really exist.

"Rather smart, aren't they?" said young Platitude. "What I mean to say, they're straight from the shoulder. Nothing people like so much as hard hitting."

He took the slips off without waiting for an answer. A few days afterwards he told me that he feared he had been too outspoken, for the weekly review had not used them; he mentioned rather bitterly that most papers were edited by their advertisement managers, and that there existed no place in journalism for a man with opinions of his own. This is the oddest thing about young Platitude. He really believes that he is a reckless iconoclast; has really convinced himself that he is a thinker of the most daring school, that he is one leading men ingeniously and without allowing them to become aware of the fact. To a meeting the other day in a Grosvenor Square drawing-room for the purpose of urging marriage reforms upon the thoughtless natives of the recently discovered country called Barala, Platitude was taken by a delightful young lady. Young Platitude found himself called upon to move a vote of thanks to the chair.

"If I may be allowed to make suggestion," said young Platitude, in his earnest, impressive way, "it is this. That our scheme of—er—reform should not be too large and not be"—here he paused—"and not be too small."

The noble Lord in the chair, in seizing upon this invaluable suggestion, complimented Platitude on his acumen, adding a phrase about old heads on young shoulders; the delightful young lady gave him a smile of reverence mixed with affection.

And this is where young Platitude scores.

WILLIAM PETT RIDGE – A SHORT BIOGRAPHY

William Pett Ridge was born at Chartham, near Canterbury, Kent, on 22nd April 1859.

His family's resources were certainly limited. His father was a railway porter, and the young Pett Ridge, after schooling in Marden, Kent became a clerk in a railway clearing-house. The hours were long and arduous, but self-improvement was Pett Ridge's goal. After working from nine until seven o'clock he would attend evening classes at Birkbeck Literary and Scientific Institute and then to follow his passion; the ambition to write. He was heavily influenced by Dickens and several critics thought he had the capability to be his successor.

From 1891 many of his humourous sketches were published in the St James's Gazette, the Idler, Windsor Magazine and other literary periodicals of the day.

Pett Ridge published his first novel in 1895, A Clever Wife. By the advent of his fifth novel, Mord Em'ly, a mere three years later in 1898, his success was obvious. His writing was written from the perspective of those born with no privilege and relied on his great talent to find humour and sympathy in his portrayal of working class life.

Today Pett Ridge and other East End novelists including Arthur Nevinson, Arthur Morrison and Edwin Pugh are being grouped together as the Cockney Novelists.

In 1924, Pugh set out his recollections of Pett Ridge from the 1890s: "I see him most clearly, as he was in those days, through a blue haze of tobacco smoke. We used sometimes to travel together from Waterloo to Worcester Park on our way to spend a Saturday afternoon and evening with H. G. Wells. Pett Ridge does not know it, but it was through watching him fill his pipe, as he sat opposite me in a stuffy little railway compartment, that I completed my own education as a smoker... Pett Ridge had a small, dark, rather spiky moustache in those days, and thick, dark, sleek hair which is perhaps not quite so thick or dark, though hardly less sleek nowadays than it was then".

With his success, on the back of his prolific output and commercial success, Pett Ridge gave generously of both time and money to charity. In 1907 he founded the Babies Home at Hoxton. This was one of several organisations that he supported that had the welfare of children as their mission.

His circle considered Pett Ridge to be one of life's natural bachelors. In 1909 They were rather surprised therefore when he married Olga Hentschel.

As the 1920's arrived Pett Ridge added to his popularity with the movies. Four of his books were adapted into films.

Pett Ridge now found the peak of his fame had passed. Although he still managed to produce a book a year he was falling out of fashion and favour with the reading public and his popularity declined rapidly. His canon runs to over sixty novels and short-story collections as well as many pieces for magazines and periodicals.

William Pett Ridge died, on 29th September 1930, at his home, Ampthill, Willow Grove, Chislehurst, at the age of 71.

He was cremated at West Norwood on 2nd October 1930.

Minor Dialogues (1895)
A Clever Wife (1895)
An Important Man and Others (1896)
Second Opportunity of Mr Staplehurst (1896)
Mord Em'ly (1898)
Outside The Radius. Stories of a London suburb (1899)
A Son of the State (1899)
A Breaker of Laws (1900)
London Only. A Set Of Common Occurrences (1901)
Lost Property (1902)
Up Side Streets – Short Stories (1903)
Erb (1903)
George And The General (1904)
Next Door Neighbours (1904)
Mrs Galer's Business (1905)
The Wickhamses (1906)
Name of Garland (1907)
Speaking Rather Seriously (1908)
Sixty Nine Birnam Road (1908)
Table d'Hôte. Tales (1910)
Splendid Brother (1910)
From Nine to Six-Thirty (1910)
Light Refreshment (1911)
Thanks to Sanderson (1911)
Love at Paddington (1912)
Devoted Sparkes (1912)
The Remington Sentence (1913)
Mixed Grill (1913)
The Happy Recruit (1914)
The Kennedy People (1915)
Book Here – Short Stories (1915)
Stray Thoughts from W. Pett Ridge (1916)
Madam Prince (1916)
The Amazing Years (1917)
Special Performance (1918)
Well To Do Arthur (1920)
Just Open. Short Stories (1920)
Richard Triumphant (1922)
Lunch Basket – Tales (1923)
Miss Mannering (1923)
Rare Luck (1924)
Leaps And Bounds (1924)
A Story Teller – Forty Years In London (1923)
Just Like Aunt Bertha (1925)
I Like To Remember (1925)
Our Mr Willis (1926)

London Types Taken From Life (1926)
Easy Distances (1927)
The Two Mackenzies (1928)
The Slippery Ladder (1929)
Eldest Miss Collingwood (1930)
Led by Westmacott (1931)

William Pett Ridge also wrote a play titled "Four small plays".

www.ingramcontent.com/pod-product-compliance
Lightning Source LLC
Chambersburg PA
CBHW021934170626
46807CB00007B/3110